BIRTH OF THE BUTTERFLY

MIMI MILAN

EATON HOUSE

BIRTH OF THE BUTTERFLY

True strength is like a sword - born of struggles forged in fire.

MIMI MILAN

Birth of the Butterfly

© 2019 by Michele Claudio

This book is a work of fiction. Names, characters, businesses, organizations, places, events and incidents either are the product of the author's imagination or are used fictitiously. Any resemblance to actual persons, living or dead, events, or locales is entirely coincidental.

Cover design by Carpe Librum Book Design.

❀ Created with Vellum

Happy Ever After to this book, I sure had my doubts at times!! If you're up for some creativity in the kitchen, you'll love this book!! I'm looking forward to reading more of Mimi's books!

~ Cindy Nipper, Reader ~

A Rebel in Jericho

"I thoroughly enjoyed A Rebel in Jericho. I felt that it was a great read. The plot was interesting and kept me turning the pages to find out what would happen next. The characters were well developed and interesting. I enjoyed the historical aspect and the description at the end of real events hinted at in the story. I like that the ending lends itself well to a sequel while effectively completing this story. I can't wait to read more by this author. I love that 20 percent of the sales from this book goes toward stop- ping human trafficking which is a bigger problem than we realize."

~ Carrie, Reader ~

"A Rebel in Jericho has a little of everything for its readers to enjoy. Suspense, romance, deception, and the desire to survive. Catalina has an incredible strength within herself, while at the same time showing just how vulnerable she is. I was intrigued to find out what twist and turns would take place next with every page I turned. I look forward to continuing reading this series and what other adventures are to come."

~ Warrior Ground ~

Twice Redeemed

I believe that this story is worth every bit of a five-star rating. It's worthy of winning a literary award."

~ Writer at Heart ~

This second book in the series is as good as the first. The characters are believable and well-written. Kind hearted former sheriff John Durbin needs to rescue the young woman who previously helped him. Will their relationship become more than rescuer and lady in danger? I recommend this book and the entire series.

~ Marianne Spitzer, Author ~

The Angel Paws Rescue series
"I really enjoyed all three of the novellas in this series (the Angel Paws Rescue series). Each novella is surprisingly very different from the other, but each has a wounded veteran

and an arts person as the hero and heroine with a pet/service animal adopted from Angel Paws Rescue. I recommend the series to anyone who enjoys clean, heart-warming contemporary romance."

~ MH, Reader ~

~ For Maki ~

I hope Japan was everything you wished for.

ACKNOWLEDGMENTS

.

When I first started writing with the Brides of Blessings series, I knew only one thing to be true. For all the numerous westerns (especially historical westerns) out on the market, very few depicted the west as it had really been—with an amazing array of characters from all walks of life. Sure, every now and then there would be a "cowboy and Indian" love story. However, the indigenous in those books rarely played a significant role (or they played a very stereotypical one). I wanted to address that. I wanted to show that people of all ethnicities and religious backgrounds helped settle the "Wild West." Hence, my characters were born. Well, almost all my characters were born. As some of you may have read in the last book, there was a character by the name of Emily Potts. She is briefly mentioned in this one as well (couldn't leave the readers hanging). However, she was actually supposed to have her own story and be the one to solve the mystery of the dragon claw necklace. Unfortunately, the group ruled that it was time to end the set. So, I had to rework my original arching plot. That led to this book, Birth of the Butterfly. It was a major wrench thrown in the clockwork, but we all managed to survive, thanks in part for all the following who helped make it possible.

Patricia Highton, you are the grammar girl extraordinaire. Thank you for pointing out when I write ridiculous sentences like "She eyes were the color of sand and sea" instead of "Her eyes were the color..." You get my drift. Considering how much I dislike the editing process, none of this would happen without you. Thanks for being my editor!

To the MFA Department in Creative Writing at Queens University of Charlotte, thank you for understanding what makes a writer tick, and for providing a lenient schedule so that I can have the day job and still pursue a writing career.

To the family and friends who have finally accepted why I disappear into my cave (and for those who don't understand, but respect what I do anyway), thank you. I owe everyone a phone call (and maybe some cake).

Finally, thank you to all the wonderful readers who have followed the series, and have gone on to pick up copies of my other books. You all give me a reason to keep writing!

lessings, CA
April 1854

"THAT'S GOING to be one lucky horse," Shin said as he penciled down the order.

Miguel Santiago, a local logger for the local wood mill, Arroyo's Lumber, looked stumped. "Sorry, Mr. Bushido, but I don't quite follow your line of thinking. What do you mean that it'll be a lucky horse?"

It was the blacksmith's turn to be confused. In the two years he served as apprentice to the former owner, he had always heard his "master" say as much to other clients. "Isn't there some saying you cowboys have about a horse shoe being lucky?" Shin asked.

Miguel chuckled. "Well, there is that. I think the luck has more to do with the fact that the horse is shoed, though. That is, you're lucky if you've got enough money to pay for them." He laughed. "The horse is the one who's lucky!"

"Oh, no." Shin nervously set down the pad he had calculated figures on. He wanted... No. He *needed* to be paid for his work. Otherwise, it would set a bad precedent. He didn't want people in town thinking he would work for free. However, he also couldn't afford to be too forceful and possibly lose a customer. Already, too many of the townsfolk questioned if they should do business with a "Chinaman." It irritated him to hear such a slur—especially since he wasn't Chinese. Only a handful of people understood the difference. The majority figured Japan... China... it was all the same. He took in a deep breath, willing himself to remain poised. If he had to lose money, then so be it. "Mr. Santiago, I'm sure we can come to some sort of arrangement if you're unable to afford the payment."

"What?" Miguel shook his head. "I think you might be under the wrong impression. I didn't mean I couldn't pay you."

Shin let out a notable sigh of relief. He gave his customer a half smile. "I'm afraid my English isn't always the best."

"Sounds just fine to me—better than my Spanish and I'm half Mexican. Why, my wife is always on my back about learning to speak better. Said it would help tremendously if I could communicate with more folks." Miguel grew solemn. "Mostly, though, I think she's still a bit sore that I couldn't help find her little brother."

Shin shook his head. "What do you mean?"

"Well, it's no secret. Surely, you heard about when the little Dayal boy, Jagara, went missing. He wasn't even a year old."

Shin scanned his thoughts. He slowly nodded. "Yes. I believe I do recall an evening when my master ranted about the world turning from bad to worse. He said something about a child abducted in a nearby town."

"Yeah, that was her brother. Half, to be precise. Born out of her daddy's second marriage."

Shin bowed slightly. "You have my condolences and deepest regret."

"Thanks, friend. If your sentiment is even half of what I feel, then I know you mean it... and I appreciate that."

"You say that as if you're guilty. Why? You did nothing wrong."

"Not everyone sees it that way," Miguel admitted. "You see, I received a letter shortly after the child went missing. I don't know if it's because it was in Spanish, or if it's more because the handwriting was so fancy, but I couldn't read it all. I did pick up a few words, though. Jagara's name, and the words 'child' and 'jewel.' I knew that it was important and rode home as fast as I could. Figured I'd give it to my wife and let her decipher it properly." He shook his head with disappointment. "What a dummy. I should have just let one of the hands at the mill translate it for me, instead of worrying about everyone knowing my business and what people would think. Then I would have known what the letter said."

"Why couldn't you know what it said anyway? Couldn't your wife translate it?"

"Sure, she could have—if I hadn't lost it."

Shin frowned. He could see how easily such a mistake could cause problems in one's marriage. It was yet another reason that he was grateful to be single. Alone meant having no one to answer to... and no one you could accidentally harm.

He looked around his shop. The man had already ordered horseshoes, and he seemed intent on paying—which he completely understood. More than likely, he would feel obligated to him as if he owed him for something. Still, it would be good business to extend some kindness. An idea dawned on him and he smiled. "Sir, does your wife like jewelry?"

Miguel looked at him curiously. "That's an interesting question. I'd say not particularly, because she doesn't wear much. But she does have a necklace she wears every day. It's the strangest thing, really. A silver dragon's claw with a bit of gold, holding a ruby that's been smoothed into a rather large round ball. To be honest, I've been thinking about getting her a ring. It's something we weren't quite in a position to do when we married due to all the upheaval." Miguel scratched his chin, his eyes glazed over with a far-off look. He blinked hard and looked at the blacksmith once more. "Why do you ask?"

Shin smiled broadly. "I offer a gift to make the wife happy. I will craft a ring of equal beauty to match that of the necklace."

"Eh, I'm not so sure. I kind of gave all my land back home to the field hands. Thought they deserved it more. Then there was the baby... now there's another on the way. Well, you know what I'm saying. I'm not so sure I should be spending any extra money on things like jewelry. I mean, I'm not sure Araceli would even want me to."

"No, you misunderstand me. This is not only a gift from you to her. You do not need to spend any money at all. This is a gift from me to your family. Consider it the beginning of our friendship."

Miguel sputtered. "I—well, now—I honestly don't know what to say. Thank you. Thank you kindly. It might take some doing to get it from her, but I'll bring the necklace by sometime. That way you can get a good look at it."

"Very good," Shin said. He picked up the horseshoes and handed them to Miguel, who then handed him a couple of bills. "Until later, best of luck to you... and the horses."

CHAPTER 1

*M*eanwhile in Acapulco, Mexico...

THE AIR WAS crisp with a sign of rain on the horizon. However, Mariposa Sanchez Tanaka paid no mind to the weather. She was centered, focused. Her dark hair tied back in the usual loose bun, thin wisps escaped to frame her square face so that her chin didn't look as strong and stubborn as the woman who owned them. She breathed in deeply, fighting hard to bring her emotions back under control. It was of no use. Her eyes snapped open and she glared at her mother.

"Why won't you just teach me?"

"Such women do not exist—especially in a country like this one," her mother calmly replied, the accent of her country still strong... and so different from her daughter's Mexican tongue. "I have explained this more than once. Why can't you understand?"

It was true. Her mother had explained it more than once.

Since the day Mariposa, little more than ten-years-old at the time, stumbled upon the sacred scrolls hidden in a sack of her mother's precious rice flour, she had made the same excuse about the parchment being little more than a musing hobby of wayward writing. She had said it so many times, in fact, that the excuse had turned into a mantra etched in Mariposa's head. It didn't matter how many times she asked —even begged—her mother to please, please teach her the ways of the warrior women. Her mother always rejected any association to the samurai's lesser known counterpart. She denied their very existence.

"The Kunoichi are a bedtime story for little children and people with no faith. There's no such thing. They don't exist."

"No, they don't exist for you! Why are you so determined to deny your strength? To pretend you can't be more than this." Mariposa waved her arms around, agitated to see the many piles of dirty laundry littering the small yard in front of their plain adobe home. "You're no longer a slave. Why do you still insist on living like one?"

Anger flashed in her mother's eyes, but it was fleeting. She sighed, reconciled to the work at hand. "There is nothing wrong with earning an honest wage. Perhaps you should try doing that instead of chasing fancies. Find a good husband. Settle down and give me grandchildren."

Mariposa snorted. "And become a different kind of slave? Not for all the riches in the world."

Her mother's face was an expressionless mask. Sure the conversation was over, Mariposa turned to leave. Her mother found her voice then, quiet yet firm. "Not all marriages are like that, Mari. Some are real."

Yeah... a real danger.

Mariposa thought about her uncle, her mother's brother, Juzo. He had fallen in love with a young Mexican woman. However, her family disapproved. He was too poor. "Bad breeding," they said. Still, the young couple could not stop seeing one another, meeting in secret until they finally found a priest who took pity on them. They thought her parents would accept him into the family once the vows were exchanged, but her parents held fast to their backwards beliefs. Even the birth of a child didn't change their minds. They forbade him to even visit the house; claimed the child as their own. Distraught, Graciela exchanged food for sadness and her body eventually grew too weak to go on. Juzo couldn't bare it any longer and convinced her to do a thing Mariposa never even knew existed until the day they pulled husband, wife and child from the lake.

Shinju.

Very little Japanese was spoken to the younger community. Their parents were much like her own mother, determined they learn the language of Spaniard nobles who had claimed Mexico, just like they had taken the few Asian women bound by chains and transported by boat. Men like her own father, who she knew very little of. So, she learned Spanish instead. This one word, though, spread through their community much like the fires that had nearly burned down the entire city. Though it happened several decades before she was even born, the people continued to nurse the trauma in every day dealings. Amidst bustling ports promising gold and new trade, men fought for power. Rebellions swelled and threatened to spill into the path of both innocents and worldly alike. The difference between the two, for as far as Mariposa could tell, was that the latter had the strength to survive.

"Imagine the power a trained woman wields," she tried convincing her mother once more. "She would be as strong as a rock."

Her mother smiled. "Even a rock must obey the sea." She wrung the last shirt and tossed it into a nearby basket. She stood and squared her shoulders, determination setting into withered lines around eyes that betrayed her. She looked exhausted. "A woman can be strong in other ways, my child. Stop running around like a wild beast. Brush your hair and find a husband."

"Like Graciela—"

"An obedient daughter does not talk back," her mother snapped, her voice cold and hard.

The words left a sour taste in Mari's mouth. She had crossed the line and knew it. Shame burned on her face for so carelessly mentioning the dead... but so did anger. She may have looked like her mother, but she was obviously nothing like her with this meek and tender persona her mother had adopted. When had her mother become so weak?

"Things would be different if my father were here," Mariposa mumbled.

"I very much doubt that." Her mother picked up the basket of clothes and started to walk away before briefly calling over her shoulder. "I have tea to make. Go do something with yourself. You look as though you've seen the ancestors."

The remark was meant to rebuke, and she knew that because it had been many years—since before Mariposa had learned to read or write—that her mother had converted to the "new way," the way of the Christians. Seeing a kami now would be a bad thing, because no festivals had been held for them, no lighting of the lanterns for many years. They would be angry at being forgotten, and do their best to wreak havoc. Mariposa could only imagine what a person who met an angry ancestor would look like. No doubt, less than becoming.

She turned and marched back towards the house, knowing there was no point in saying anything further to her mother. You couldn't argue with air... and that's what her mother always did whenever they disagreed. She'd say her piece and then walk away, leaving Mariposa to "huff" with frustration and walk off in the opposite direction—in this case, the house. She stormed off to the bedroom—the one she shared with her mother—only to find a cousin there. She sighed.

"Chuya, what are you doing here?"

She rummaged through a basket of old clothes that Mariposa's mother no longer wore. "What does it look like I'm doing?"

"Trying to take more of my mother's garments without permission."

"For your information, I asked this time. She said I was welcomed to take the blue kimono... and what bee stung you today? Storming in here and acting like I've committed some crime. I've done nothing wrong and yet you accuse me like some beggar in the streets," her cousin gushed out all her thoughts in one breath.

Mariposa shrugged. "You're right. I shouldn't have spoken so harshly. My fight isn't with you."

"Really, Mari, you shouldn't have a fight with anyone. Who in this town is your enemy?"

Mariposa froze. The idea of her mother as an enemy was the last impression she wanted to create. Yes, they had their differences. However, they most certainly weren't enemies. "Perhaps fight was too strong a word. I think disagreement might be more a bit more appropriate."

"Ah, let me guess. You and auntie aren't seeing eye to eye?"

"You could say that."

"And what is it this time?" Chuya smirked. "Did you spill the tea again?"

Mariposa sighed at the reminder of yet another way she

9

disappointed her mother. She was forever trying to impress upon Mariposa the importance of the traditional tea ceremonies—one of the only traditions she did keep from before. Not because she wanted her to learn anything about the culture of her ancestors, but because it was one more thing that could impress a potential husband.

"It has nothing to do with tea," Mariposa said. "She doesn't seem to understand that I don't want to be bound to some man."

Truth be told, the only man she wanted to chase after was the kind who had a big bounty on his head—the bigger, the better. Then maybe she would have enough money to replace the inheritance she had lost. Not that she was entirely sure the necklace had been worth all that much money to begin with, but her mother had certainly led her to believe so. That was the only reason she had gotten away without having to marry for so long. When she had lost it in an ill-begotten game of cards, her mother was so furious that she actually wept. Mariposa couldn't recall a time in her life she had seen her mother cry—not even when Uncle passed. The hope of one day figuring out the necklace's puzzle of secret wealth slipped away as swiftly as he had.

"What is wrong with finding a good husband?" Her cousin's shrewd voice broke into Mariposa's thoughts. "You are not so pretty, but you could do alright."

Mariposa frowned. She knew she wasn't the most beautiful girl in town. However, she was still prettier than Chuya. That much she was certain of. She also knew that her cousin was simply trying to get under her skin for the implication of being called a thief—a serious crime that could result in a whipping (or worse) if found out by the wrong crowd. Still, she wasn't about to let someone like Chuya talk down to her.

"Who are you to criticize anyone?" Mariposa challenged. "We both know why you paint your face."

It was a cheap remark to make. It wasn't Chuya's fault that a bull had broken out of its fence and terrorized the town for nearly twenty minutes, stopping only after the owner could see no other way to return order and finally gave the men permission to kill it. Unfortunately, one of them had taken to his drink early in the day. He was hardly for shooting that day—made apparent by the bullet that had whizzed through the marketplace, past the Tanaka women, to completely miss its mark only after grazing Chuya's cheek. She had the same look of surprise and dismay then as she did now.

Chuya swallowed hard. "What do you know about life? You're just a silly girl."

Mariposa sighed. "I'm sorry, Chuya. I shouldn't have said—"

Her cousin whirled around and stormed out of the room, slamming the door shut before Mariposa could finish her apology. Sinking on the bed, Mariposa moaned. Her cousin was right. Twenty-two and with no matches to make, she still had a lot to learn. Amongst her chief shortcomings was the inability to keep her tongue in check. Her mother was always saying it would get her in trouble one day, and she couldn't help but feel that one day would be someday soon.

She lay back on the bed and stared up at the dirt ceiling, contemplating the various things she could do to make amends with both her mother and cousin—neither of whom she liked fighting with. They were, in fact, the only real family she had left with so many others either dead, sent back to Spain like her own father, or off politicking for Antonio Lopez de Santa Anna. She had no personal opinion of the man herself. However, she couldn't see what good would come of supporting a man who had been in exile after defeat in the war against Americans, a person welcomed back only after a group of churchmen had successfully overthrown the government. Surely, this would only lead to yet more fighting.

Perhaps if she had been born a man...

Or if mother would teach me the ways of the Kunoichi.

She could imagine it now—drawing her sword and fighting alongside the men. Not that she had a sword. Still, she could imagine it all. The battle began in her mind, the general calling her to join beside him. She proudly rode up to face their enemy—yet another foreign invader who wanted to sell their men into slavery and take their women as mistresses and maids. She let out a loud battle cry.

"Girl!"

Mariposa shot up, jumping off the bed to face her mother.

"Why are you screaming like that?"

"I must have dozed off—had a bad dream," Mariposa lied.

Her mother frowned, but said nothing more about any concerns she may have had. "Come to the sitting room. There is something we must discuss."

It was Mariposa's turn to look less than pleased—which most certainly wasn't when she followed her mother out of the small quarters they shared and into the room that served to welcome guests. The nicest room in the house, it was the only one with any real furniture—two chairs with woven seats opposite to a plush settee adjacent to the long wall. A small wooden table separated the furnishings... and the two women, fashionably dressed, sat on the sofa cushions while she and her mother took the less fashionable chairs. One looked like a slightly older version of her mother, but much more refined, with her hair pulled back in a bun and face made up like the western women Mariposa has occasionally seen at the port, traveling with their spouses or even bravely conducting business as if equal to a man. This woman appeared to be that very sort. Her kimono was strangely short—much shorter than Mariposa had ever seen before—

and she wore men's slacks beneath it as if her very wardrobe commanded respect. The other woman was much more feminine, as well as distinctive of where she hailed from. A traditional mantilla of fine Spanish lace hung from an ornate comb in her hair. It draped down across her shoulders like a fine, thin shawl.

Mariposa's mother bowed her head slightly. "Welcome to our home, Fuku-san. This is my daughter, Mariposa Sanchez Tanaka. Mariposa, this is Madam Fuku."

"Sanchez," the older woman repeated. "That is interesting."

"She was given the father's name, in honor of his people."

"An honor... or a reminder?"

Mariposa didn't quite follow the woman's line of questioning, but knew it must have been grave. Her mother's face darkened (with embarrassment or anger her daughter couldn't be sure). Some unspoken affront had been committed, though. Mariposa gently cleared her throat. "Madam Fuku, you honor us," she spoke in Japanese, knowing her accent was wrong and the words stilted. Still, she tried her best to appease the woman who seemed of greater authority than her own mother.

The woman smiled slightly, a tight smile that seemed as grim as the situation at hand. Mariposa had seen the woman before. She was sure of it. She just couldn't remember from where.

"Thank you," the woman responded. "However, I think we will need to find a language that suits us all. Do you speak English?"

"I do."

"Good," the woman said, easily switching languages. "Naturally, Dona Ramirez does not speak Japanese," the woman motioned to her companion. "And, sadly enough, I have spent more time with Americans than I have in your... fair... pueblo. Therefore, I have not yet mastered Spanish."

Mariposa's mother took control of the conversation once more. "Yes. It has been some years since you last visited us. I hope your voyage was pleasant."

"It was what it was."

"I understand. Please, allow us to welcome you properly. My daughter will pour the tea."

The woman nodded her approval. "Very well. Let us get right down to business then."

All eyes turned to Mariposa, expectant of her to obviously do something. Her mother chuckled nervously. "I'm afraid you'll have to excuse my daughter. I failed to tell her we had guests coming." Her mother turned and gave her a little shove, seemingly harmless to any peering eyes. However, the warning tone in her mother's voice succinctly delivered the message. "The tea I mentioned earlier? It is in the kitchen. Bring it for our guests."

Part of Mariposa wanted to refuse, but a little voice inside told her it would be the wrong thing to do. While she didn't exactly want to play the role of "good hostess," she could imagine how much more difficult life would be if her mother's mood turned truly cantankerous. Not that her mother was abusive in any way, but simply that she could make life difficult. Even now, Mariposa knew she had it good, with her mother cooking most of the meals and taking care of the house. Compared to others her age—women forced to marry if they were lucky, or become street walkers if they weren't—she got to be wild and carefree for the most part. She was thankful for that. Besides, there was something about the women that sent alarm through Mariposa. She didn't know either one, but could tell they were not to be toyed with.

It's only a cup of tea. You can do that much. Right?

Of course she could! With a smile, too. Then maybe the

woman would be pleased. That, in turn, would please her mother. Perhaps enough to give Mariposa the one thing she wanted... a complete translation of the documents she so dearly wanted to understand. She smiled to herself. Yes, this plan was certain to work. How could her mother say "no" in front of such important guests anyway? She would want to show herself agreeable and pleasing.

Elated, Mariposa hummed a little as she chose the finest wooden tray they owned and pulled out a pretty set of clay cups. They were crafted in a fine Talavera style, with Monarch butterflies floating above delicate flowers. It was one of the few things of any value that her father had left them. Well, that and the necklace. She sighed, forlorn to have been so foolish, but then gave her head a firm shake. She wouldn't dwell on any of that right now. She would serve the tea... and change her fortune in other ways.

Careful... careful.

Mariposa carried the tray into the room, sending up a prayer to the God she had learned about at the local Catholic church—the one her mother didn't believe in herself, but insisted that her daughter attend.

Please don't let me drop this tray.

Her mind flashed back to the day of her Uncle's funeral. Distracted, she hadn't seen an attendee standing behind her and bumped into him. He tried to catch her, but she swung around and ended up spilling hot tea all over him. She sighed. That was an embarrassment she certainly didn't want to relive—especially since her mother used it as an example to not teach her the *ninpo*. Who could learn to balance well in a fighting stance if they couldn't even balance a tray of tea?

She placed the tray on the table, picked up a cup, placed it in front of the woman and scooped herbs into it.

"English tea?" The woman gave them a questioning look. "You are full of surprises, Tanaka Chie."

15

Mariposa looked to her mother, unaccustomed to hearing anyone say her given name last. Why did she not show more respect and say "San" as well?

"I thought it best, as we are speaking the language."

The woman smirked. "Ah, but you would not have known that I'd request we speak it."

"I could not be certain, no. However, I had anticipated such when I learned of who traveled with you." She nodded at Dona Ramirez.

The woman allowed her the small win. "Very wise. I see you have lived up to your name." The victory was short-lived. "It's a shame you did not show such foresight in regards to your finances."

Her mother frowned, but said nothing. Emotions slowly roiling within her, Mariposa stared at the woman who had raised her, the woman who always seemed so strong. How could she sit here now and simply take this woman's snide remarks? A low growl sounded from Mariposa's throat, and her anger boiled over before she could stop.

"How dare you speak to my mother like that... and in her own home!" Forget accidentally spilling tea on someone. This lady was lucky if she didn't throw it at her! Mariposa raised a shaky finger. "Leave this house at once"

The woman smiled broadly. She glanced over to her companion, who wore her own small smile and nodded approvingly.

"She will do," Dona Ramirez said.

Mariposa's mother bolted from her chair. "No! I will not allow it. You cannot have my daughter."

"Allow? My dear, you forget your place."

They may not have always seen eye to eye, but Mariposa knew well that loyalty to family was honorable, and honor was everything. More so now than ever before as it was obvious her mother was trying to protect her from something. She stepped forward, ready to fight the whole world if need be. "No one has forgotten anything. This is our place. Do you understand? You are the one who is a guest in our home. A guest who has worn out her welcome. Leave before I call for the authorities."

"Ah, but you see, that is where you're wrong." Madam Fuku calmly folded her hands and placed them on her lap. "I realize now that your mother has failed in not only advising you as to who was coming to visit today, but why we have come." The woman looked serenely at her mother then. "Will you tell her, Tanaka Chie, or shall I?"

Mariposa's mother looked from one woman to the next, their expressions vulture-like, as if conspicuously waiting to dive right into easy pickings. Her mother sighed.

"This is not really our home."

Mariposa shook her head, confused. "What do you mean? I've lived here my entire life. Father built us this home."

Her mother nodded. "Yes, that's right. Your father did build this home. However, he didn't really build it for us."

That feeling of rising alarm coursed through her once again. "Well, if not for us, then for whom did he build it?"

Chie took in a slow breath. "For his wife."

"What are you talking about?" Mariposa shook her head, refusing to understand. "You are his wife."

"No, I'm not." Chie turned to the two women, gruffly addressing them. "Please excuse us."

In a rare moment of desperation, Chie grabbed her daughter's hand and dragged her through the house, out the back door and into the privacy of their small garden. She took a moment to compose herself, breathing in deeply the smell of Cempasuchil flowers. Their gold and red petals—the same colors of the dragon claw necklace Mariposa once sported—evoking the same emotions of dying promise in both women. They had wanted for so much, but received so little.

Her mother finally addressed her. "Mariposa, you must understand. Where I come from, it was very normal for a man to have more than one wife. That is why I said 'yes' when your father proposed to me. I knew of Dona Ramirez —had seen them walking together in the marketplace. I didn't think much of her, though. She seemed a beautiful, but cold woman. When he pursued me, I thought it was because she could not bear him children." Her mother sighed. "I was wrong."

She was shocked to hear her father had been married to another, but even more disturbed by the idea that she might have siblings somewhere out in the world and that she had never known of it. "He had other children?"

"Yes. Dona Ramirez had her child—a son—the year after I had you." Her mother suddenly looked thoughtful, her eyes filming over with a thin mist that usually accompanies memories. "Like, I said. Things are different in Japan. Most husbands with more than one wife would have them both sleep under the same roof. However, that was not always the case. Some men were wealthy enough to own more than one home. Your father was certainly one of those men. Building this home here... buying all sorts of materials so that I could raise you proper. He was always so apologetic for his frequent absences. I was always understanding. I knew that would keep him kind and generous, and it did... for a while. Then his wife learned of what transpired between us. Oh, she was furious. She was so mad that she insisted they move immediately."

"And father left? Just like that?"

"Of course he did. Though not directly related to royalty, his family is of noble blood. They would have never permitted a marriage annulment, let alone marriage to one of their servants."

"Why didn't you do something?" Mariposa demanded. "Why didn't you try to stop him?"

"I did do something. I asked for two things. Honestly, I thought you and I could get on well enough without him if we had that much."

"What did you ask for?"

"First, I asked for my freedom from Madam Fuku."

"Madam Fuku?" Mariposa asked, surprised. She had always known of the difficulties her mother had faced. However, she hadn't been aware that the very person who caused it all was proudly sitting in their home, sipping cherry blossom tea.

Her mother nodded. "Yes, it was she who brought me here—all the way from Japan. I'll be honest. My parents were only too happy for it, and so was I."

Mariposa didn't know her maternal grandparents—not even from a painting. Still, she couldn't imagine any parent wanting their child to be sold into slavery. "How could you think you would be happy serving others?"

"Oh, I wasn't happy serving others. At least, not in that sense," her mother explained. "The truth is that I didn't know exactly what to expect. My parents had arranged with Madam Fuku that I would be allowed to earn my freedom one day. She agreed and a sum was put in place to cover my passage to America. But first I had to work off the money she had loaned my parents to pay off their own debts."

"Was it a lot?"

"Not so much on their own. The real debt came from my travels, as well as my keep."

"Your keep?"

"Yes, there was a charge for everything. From the clothes on my back to the barn roof over my head, and even my meals. Madame Fuku accounted for everything—even down to the last grain of rice. Even a sip of water had a price on it."

"How could anyone ever pay off such debts?"

"That's why many of us went without baths. You can imagine how much such a luxury would cost." Her mother shrugged, her face pained with sadness. "Now you know why I let your father go without a fight. Not only did I not have much claim to him as little more than a second wife, but I very badly wanted my freedom. So, he paid off all my debts to Madame Fuku. Then he made me the promise of providing a way for you to one day have more than I ever could."

Mariposa gasped with sudden understanding. "The dragon claw necklace."

"Yes," her mother said. "The necklace. At first, I didn't think he would hold true to his word. That wouldn't have been the end of the world, of course, but it would have made me very disappointed to see you in a position like the one I had come to know. Then, about eight years after he left, he sent a messenger with a strange gift. It was a sack of rice flour that contained two items hidden within it."

Mariposa's eyes lit up. "The parchment!"

"Yes, that was one of the items."

"But that would mean…"

Mariposa frowned.

"That is correct," Chie confirmed her daughter's unspoken suspicions. "The document you found referring to the Kunoichi didn't belong to me. Not originally. I was never some warrior woman."

Mariposa shook her head. "No. That's not possible."

Chie grabbed her daughter's hands. She affectionately ran a hand down Mariposa's face. "It is true. I'm sorry, child. I wish I could have been the woman you wanted—a woman worthy of your fierce spirit. I was never a fighter, though. I did as I was told—what was expected and even demanded of me. However, I will not make that mistake now. I will fight for you until my last breath. They will never take you from me."

Tears filled Mariposa's eyes. "What are you talking about? Take me? Why are those women even here?"

Her mother sighed. "Mari, when your father passed away, his son inherited everything... including this house. Except he doesn't want this house. His mother does."

Mariposa slowly nodded, understanding what her mother was trying to explain. "And she's here to collect. Not so much because she has to, but because she wants to."

Her mother's head hung with embarrassment. "Yes."

Mariposa thought for a moment. "What did that woman say? Something about how I would do?"

Her mother waved away the concern. "It will not happen. I won't allow you to work off my debts."

"What debts are you talking about? How do you owe that woman money?"

"I don't owe her, per se. I owed your father. Well, not really owed." Her mother sighed once more. "Your father always kept meticulous track of his finances. He wrote every little thing down. If he spent money, or even gave it to someone, he would write it down in his books."

"Did he give you money?"

"Not money. The necklace."

Mariposa moaned. Of course it would be the necklace... the one that she lost doing one of the most foolish things possible. "She wants you to pay back the necklace my father gave you?"

"The necklace... and the house."

"The house? But why? She doesn't need it. I'm sure she has another. Probably more than one."

"It doesn't matter. Her son gave her the house once he inherited it. Legally, it belongs to her."

"And the necklace?"

"His books only showed that it was given to us. It didn't specify that it was a gift."

"So now she's calculated that into the money she wants repaid?"

"Yes. She and Madame Fuku are opening a tea house in a small town in California. They wish me to serve as a maid until the debt has been repaid."

Frustrated, Mariposa swiped back an annoying wisp of hair. Her voice quivered with anger. "Mother, you will never pay back that kind of money. At your age? They will work you to death."

Her mother shrugged. "What other choice is there? I have to do what I have to do."

"No," Mariposa said. She stood a little straighter, her head held high with determination. "It is I who has to do something."

She turned and started marching back towards the house.

"What are you going to do?" Her mother called out as she ran after her.

Mariposa stopped only long enough to answer her.

"The only thing that makes sense. I'm going to take your place."

CHAPTER 2

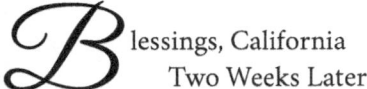 lessings, California
Two Weeks Later

"GOTTA SAY, Mr. Bushido, your work is just as good as your master's was." The man examined the set of horseshoes he had commissioned the blacksmith to make. "I'm impressed."

Shin forced a smile, disappointed that he couldn't completely appreciate the compliment. After all, he had no one to blame but himself. He was the one who had spent the last two years working as an apprentice to Mr. Willis, a man who preferred to drink himself to death more than do any actual work around the shop. Shin hadn't wanted to rock the proverbial boat, though, and had allowed the former blacksmith to present Shin's work as his own because he knew how difficult it could be to repair a reputation once it was destroyed. If there was anything he knew from his former life, then it was that much. Unfortunately, it did little good for him now that he had taken over as the new owner. It seemed like he would always have to live in someone else's shadow.

He cleared his throat and with it his mind. "Thank you, Mr. Adair. I'm sure they'll serve your horses well—all the way to Charming."

The man grinned. "Here's to hoping!"

Shin showed the man to the door. "Have a safe journey, Mr. Adair. I hope the town of Charming lives up to its name."

The gentleman handed over a few bills and said goodbye, leaving Shin alone with his thoughts once more. He stood in the threshold of the smithy, staring out at the small town of Blessings. Despite his feelings of not completely belonging, everything else was as it should be. Passersby in mid-morning conversation strolled down the road, heading towards the diner or mercantile. Horses, tethered to their posts, stomped their hoofs.

Shin turned his head. The only thing a bit out of place was all the activity going on in front of a previously aban-doned building. He glanced over his shoulder and spied the dying fire. It would be safe to leave it unattended for a bit while he went to find out more. He walked down the street, nodding at a person or two and bidding them a good day as they passed one another until he happened upon his newest friend.

"Morning, Miguel. How are things going with you and the family?"

Miguel gave him a tired smile. "I can't complain. Just wish I was getting a little more sleep is all. You wouldn't have anything for that, would you?"

Shin chuckled. "Wish I could give you some advice, but I wouldn't know anything about taking care of small children."

"Child," Miguel corrected him. "It's still only one."

"With another on the way," Shin reminded him with a huge grin. He was enjoying this friendship. It was easy.

Miguel took a steadying breath. "I know. Doesn't change the fact that I'm still nervous."

"Why would you be nervous? From what I've seen, you are a good father."

Miguel shrugged. "Well, you know how it is. Like I said back at your shop—things haven't been easy since Araceli's brother disappeared."

Shin sobered quickly. He clapped a hand down on Miguel's shoulder. "Do not borrow trouble, my friend. What happened once is unlikely to happen again."

Miguel slowly exhaled. "Yeah, I'm sure you're right. It just kind of puts the rest of us on edge. Leaves us feeling like we've always got to keep an eye out."

Shin saw an opening to change the subject and maybe get his friend's mind off of his troubles. "Speaking of keeping an eye out..." He pointed to the hustle and bustle across from them. "What's going on there?"

"Oh, there's going to be a new teahouse there."

Shin's curiosity peaked. "A teahouse? As in tea and biscuits like the English enjoy?"

"No, actually. I'd say it might be a little more along the lines of what you're used to. In fact, the woman we're delivering the lumber to is some sort of Madame come all the way from Japan."

"Really?"

"Yeah. From what I've heard, she's even brought a few special ladies with her. Mind you, nothing like you'd find in a cathouse. These women are supposed to be classy entertainers of sorts. I don't quite get it all, though. They paint their faces like ghosts."

Geisha.

Shin nodded with understanding. As more gold was found and work on the railroad commenced, more people settled in the area. That including people like himself. It was only natural that they would want to bring the traditions of home with them. Though he hoped there would be a tradition or two that would be left behind. If there was one thing he never wished to see again, it was an opium den. The dreadful stuff had wrecked enough lives—including his.

He smiled at Miguel. "Yes, it does sound familiar. Perhaps I'll go and check it out."

Miguel tipped his hat at him. "Let me know how it goes. I've got to get on with the next delivery. Then it's home for daddy duty. My turn to watch Raquel so Araceli can get a little work done. She's trying to paint a replica of the Sistine chapel. Saw the thing in a book when we went to San Diego and can't get the picture out of her mind. Now she wants to see if she can create something similar."

"Then send her my best," Shin said. "And don't forget to send the necklace along, too. I still have that ring to make."

Miguel climbed up into his wagon and snapped the horse's reigns. "Will do, partner."

Shin watched the wagon jostle down the road for a few moments, and then turned his attention back to the new teahouse. He strode over, past a few men hammering away outside, and slowly entered the building. Looking around, he could see the mix of both old world and new. Hanging on one wall were paintings of beautiful geisha. On another were Katakana characters, artistically written in black ink. However, there was an obvious difference from what he had seen in the temples back home. Where all their work—from seals to decrees and more—were placed on sturdy Xuan paper designed to last centuries, these works of art appeared to be on inferior rice paper.

Shin walked in further, ignoring a man who sanded the stair banister. He followed the sound of voices coming from beyond another room, out into the back courtyard. He was surprised to find how it had been designed with miniature bonsai trees in clay jars, and flowers (like the red Spider Lily) of which he hadn't seen in many years. However, he was even more surprised to spy a dozen or so young women sitting around, fanning themselves as they sipped their tea. The ladies chatted with one another in Japanese. He was surprised to hear how they spoke, though. Rather, he was more surprised that the one young woman they poked fun at didn't respond at all. Bent over her work at a washtub, she furiously scrubbed as the women referred to her as "*hafu*." It bordered on derogatory. Did the young woman even hail from the Ainu region of Japan? Was she really a half-breed... and who cared if she was?

More importantly, why did he care?

Because someone should say something, and who would if not him? He addressed the group of gossiping girls. "You shouldn't speak that way about others."

The women turned. Surprised to find someone in their private domain, some hid behind their fans. Others turned their backs completely, their heads dipped low to avoid eye contact. An older woman stepped forward. "I'm sorry, sir, but we are not yet open for business."

Shin frowned. "I doubt you will get very much of it if these are the kind of women meant to entertain your clients. Their tongues are as sharp as swords."

The woman bowed. "Of course, you are right. Please forgive their foolishness. They are not themselves today. Some are still in training. It is one reason why we are not yet open." She straightened and motioned to the work going on behind him, back inside the building. "As you can see, the other reason is because we are still creating the appropriate atmosphere. As I'm sure you know, it is difficult for geisha to be in such chaotic environment. The girls will be themselves once more when all has returned to normal. You will come back and see Madame Fuku's girls then, yes?"

Shin wasn't too sure he believed the Madame's excuse, but what did it really matter anyway? It wasn't like he had any real intention of visiting the tea house once it was open for business. He wasn't a wealthy man who could afford to waste money on properly served tea, and while he did enjoy listening to the Sangen, he wasn't about to pay hard earned money simply to watch a painted woman pluck away at the three stringed instrument. Although...

His eyes drifted up again, past the Madame, to the young woman who had now abandoned her wash. Her dark hair was in a loose bun that had shifted from one side to the other while she worked, allowing quite a bit of it to fall free. She pushed it back with wet, soapy hands to reveal soft, curious eyes that flitted this way and that, reminding him very much of a floating butterfly as she openly studied his face. He nodded her way, but addressed the matron who blocked his path.

"It is strange to set your geisha to labor. Are you not concerned the lye will ruin her hands?"

Madame Fuku glanced over her shoulder. "Oh, that one is not geisha yet."

"Then she is maiko?"

"Of course. Do you like her?"

Shin schooled his features, careful not to show how he felt about the strange situation. It wasn't that he didn't like her. He simply didn't know her. However, he was interested in her story. She looked to be at least twenty years of age. Yet, much like a *shikomi*, she was assigned to menial tasks. Shikomi were young girls, though. Procured from a young age of maybe six or seven, they stopped taking care of house-hold chores to start their own training as geisha several years later. So why was she in such a position of servitude? Was she that—a servant—or worse? A slave with no rights at all?

Madame Fuku cleared her throat. "I know I said we aren't

quite open yet, but I could arrange a... special... meeting if you'd like." She gave him a knowing smile. Shin only frowned. He didn't like the way this woman did business. It wasn't customary for an okiya to sell the services of its women. At least, not a reputable one.

"These women are geisha, or they are *oiran?*"

"This is a new world, and we must all do our part to survive." The Madame shrugged as if it made no difference if her establishment provided the kind of entertainment many in the town would find unsavory. "They are whatever they need to be... and they are good regardless. Perhaps the better question is what do you need? If nothing, then I offer my apologies for wasting your time. I will see you out."

There was little more Shin disliked greater than being summarily dismissed. What the Madame didn't know, though, was that he had battled far greater foes than she. He wasn't the sort to be brushed off so easily—especially seeing as to how she actually did business. Not that he was in the role of protecting people any longer. She was right. This was a new world. The rules were different here. No one was going to pay him to play savior—especially since he had failed so miserably at it before. Still, his conscience wouldn't allow him to walk away and do nothing.

"I am needing someone of a different fashion," he quickly explained. "I would like her to come clean my shop."

Madame Fuku chuckled. "That is quite impossible. She has far too many chores here."

"So many chores that she could not be of service to others now and then?"

"What can I say? She has a debt to repay."

"Do you mean to say that you would turn down good money so that she could work here for free? Could she not repay that debt faster if she earned actual money?"

"That is not the arrangement we've made. Until the debt

is repaid, she must take care of her sisters. Such is the way of the okiya. Until then, she can belong to no other."

Shin frowned. He didn't necessarily have the ear of anyone important in town, but he was familiar with the town's founder, Atherton Winslet, well enough to know he would never condone the idea of anyone belonging to another—which wasn't even his intention to begin with. Had this woman gotten some silly idea that he was looking for more than a washerwoman? Had he not specifically said it was to clean the shop? Shin inwardly sighed. He supposed it did look a bit strange. After all, it wasn't custom for men and women to mix together unchaperoned. That wasn't the message he had intended to deliver. However, who was this woman to imply such? Adamant, he crossed his arms. "Perhaps this is a matter for the law."

Madame Fuku blanched. She settled one hand on her chest, as if doing so would still the anxious beating of her heart. "The law?"

Shin nodded, satisfied that he had her full attention. "Yes. It appears you are not aware of our town's ordinances."

"What ordinances?"

"The one about keeping another in servitude."

There! He would turn the table back on her.

Madame Fuku raised her hands in defense, her expression full of confusion. "I have done nothing wrong. These arrangements are the same many men make all over the country."

"Ah, but you see we are not like the rest of the country. Mayor Atherton has made it quite clear that this is a town where men—and women—are all considered equal. It's not a popular opinion, but such progressive ways are the reason we see much less crime than other settlements."

Madame Fuku coyly rolled her shoulders. "I am not one to create discord."

Shin snorted. "I highly doubt that."

"It's true," Madame Fuku insisted. "And to show that I am an agreeable *okasan*, I will grant your wish. You may hire young Mariposa."

Mariposa?

Shin looked past the woman, her continued speech floating right past his ears as he studied the new hire that had now set the broom aside to openly study him. Her eyes were soft with curiosity at first, but locking with his own gaze turned them hard like two pieces of black coal. He suddenly felt embarrassed, concern filling him with doubt. Had there been something in his expression that alarmed her? Could she weigh and measure him so quickly, and know that he was not someone she could be safe with?

"Did you hear me?" Madame Fuku asked.

Startled, Shin nodded. "Yes," he lied. "Yes, of course."

"Good. Then we have an agreement," Madame Fuku clarified the rules once more. "You will pay for her services before she attends to your... shop." The woman said the word as if she still doubted his intentions. "Should she fail a single exam, the arrangement will end."

Exam? Shin wasn't sure he quite understood, but quickly nodded his agreement, a bit frustrated that he didn't know what he was agreeing to and that he had no one but himself to blame for becoming distracted to begin with like some wet-behind-the-ears kohai.

"Yes, that is fine."

"Very well. You have the money?"

Shin wasn't sure what amount he had agreed to, and the truth was that he didn't earn much as a blacksmith. However, he did have a small gold nugget that fit neatly in his palm. He brought it with him everywhere he went in the off-chance that some wayward delinquent broke into his shop and rob him blind. He dug into his pocket and produced it. Madame

Fuku's eyes grew as round as dinner plates, the hunger apparent in her eyes.

"Are you sure you wish to spend that much on one so unworthy? We have other women you may find more pleasing."

Shin held back a growl. Why was it this woman didn't understand that his intentions were good? "I have already stated my needs. I do not appreciate my honor being questioned."

"Oh, I would never question your honor." Madame Fuku bowed deeply. "I simply wish to convey my concerns. The woman you wish to work for you can, at times, have something of a sour disposition."

Shin glanced up at Mariposa once more. She had moved on to weeding their small vegetable garden. A small flick of her eyes confirmed his suspicions, though. She was interested in his conversation with the house mother.

He confidently smiled down at Madame Fuku. "I am not paying for her personality. I'm paying for her ability to clean —something I suspect the other ladies may not be able to accomplish. They seem far too delicate to stand the heat of an iron forge. I'm sure you wouldn't want any of them to faint from heat exhaustion."

"You make a valid point," Madame Fuku said. "You shall have Mariposa three times a week, starting this Friday. Your payments will go towards the debt she owes, beginning with this initial offer."

She held her hand out for the gold nugget. Shin hesitated.

"I don't believe we agreed on a price for this piece," he said.

Madame Fuku plucked the gold from him and weighed it in the center of her palm. She looked at him squarely. "I am a fair woman. I believe in people receiving what they pay for and getting exactly what they deserve." She glanced back down at the nugget. "This feels about half her worth."

Shin could have cringed at the way the woman described a person's worth in terms of money, but he couldn't say much. Wasn't it nearly the same as any profession? Besides, he had fought—and won—enough battles for one day. It was good to quit while ahead.

"And how many days will half her worth give me?"

"I will give you thirty days for this piece of gold."

"Thirty days? What if she doesn't do the job as entailed?"

Madame Fuku shrugged. "That is a risk you'll have to take. There is no refund once we sign the papers."

Shin glanced up once more to study the young woman. She had abandoned her task and stood half hidden behind a bonsai tree. Was that a look of hope he read in her face? She turned away too fast for him to be sure, but he was almost certain that she desired to escape the okiya as much as he wished to be of some assistance. He returned his attention to the house mother.

"I understand."

"Good. Then I will draw up the papers at once and have them delivered to your shop." Madame Fuku said. "Congratulations. I hope you know what you are doing."

Shin only nodded before turning to leave Blessings soon-to-be first teahouse. She wasn't the only one who hoped he knew what he was doing.

He did, too.

CHAPTER 3

"*W*hat was I supposed to say? No? He threatened to bring the law. That's trouble I don't need."

"Well, you could have said something. I needed her to stay here."

"I did say something—and I got good money for it, too."

Mariposa stood outside Madame Fuku's private chambers, squinting to see through the slim crack between the double doors as she listened to her "house mother" and Dona Ramirez argue. Did they know how loud they were speaking... or did they simply not care? Either way, it wasn't like she was intentionally eavesdropping. She had been instructed to "stand right there and don't move" when Dona Ramirez arrived and demanded she leave the room so the women could talk in private. What she didn't understand was why the Dona cared so much about the fact that Mariposa wouldn't be at the okiya for a few days each week. She was still getting paid. In fact, this would bring the money in much faster than simply sweeping floors or caring for the other women in the house—not all of whom, she had learned, were indeed geisha. Some of them weren't maiko, or even of Japanese heritage. They were women in the "employ" of Dona Ramirez, but Mariposa had yet to learn what purpose they served. All she knew was that she would take one or two of them with her and leave on some mission. The women would return, looking like they had rolled around in dirt for half the day. It always irritated Mariposa because she was the one who had to wash the women's clothes. Meanwhile, they were kept secluded in a private room that looked as lavish as that of the Madame's personal quarters.

The doors swung open and Dona Ramirez appeared. She grabbed Mariposa by the arm and dragged her into the room. She swung her around so fiercely, Mariposa nearly lost her balance. Dona Ramirez gruffly straightened her up. One hand still firmly gripping Mariposa's arm, she angrily shook a finger at her with the other.

"You listen to me, princesa. Make one foolish mistake and I will make your life miserable."

Mariposa snorted. She had never been anyone's "princess." She also couldn't think of anything else that would make her life more miserable than what it already was.

"Oh, you think you're so tough? You don't think I can make your life even more difficult than what it already is?"

Mariposa shrugged. "I'm sure you could. The question is whether or not I would really care."

Dona Ramirez inhaled sharply. She lifted a hand and brought it down, narrowly missing Mariposa's face when Madame Fuku jumped forward and grabbed her partner.

"No!" She held fast to the woman's wrist. "You must not damage the merchandise."

The two women stared at each other. Dona Ramirez let out a growl. She pushed her face into Mariposa's and warned her.

"Perhaps you're right. Maybe it doesn't matter what I do to you. But do you care at all for your mother?"

Mariposa gasped.

Dona Ramirez smiled triumphantly. "That's what I thought. So, no running off. Do your job and then return to me," she patted Mariposa's head, "like an obedient little *sirviente*."

Mariposa pulled away. Regardless of what this woman thought, she was nobody's servant. At least, she hadn't been born such. It didn't seem to matter much, though. That is, not at the moment. Mariposa was sitting at a table full of sharks and Dona Ramirez seemed to hold all the good cards. For this hand leastways. The day would come when she would be free of this dreadful woman—the both of them.

She looked over at Madame Fuku, surprised to find her face longer than she would have expected. Almost as if there was a trace of sadness etched along her fine wrinkles. Did the woman actually care about what happened to her? Why had she behaved so harshly with Mariposa's mother, but quickly stepped in to protect her just now? Mariposa thought to question the older woman, but Madame Fuku turned away before she could summon the courage.

"You must go now," the woman said, her back facing Mariposa. "Mr. Bushido has paid good money for your services. You must not disappoint him."

"Of course," Mariposa said. Then she spun around and left the room, snatching up a brown cloth satchel she had dropped outside the door when Dona Ramirez accosted her. Inside were instructions on where to go, as well as a bit of food for her lunch in case Mr. Bushido proved less hospitable than desired.

Mariposa walked out of the teahouse and into the brilliant sunlight that shined down on Blessings. Eyes closed, she turned her face skyward and breathed in deeply. The scents of summer filled her lungs. Hardwoods and wild flowers and dust all fought for equal attention, but ten short steps and they were all forgotten as the smell of sizzling steaks filled the air. Mariposa turned her head towards the local diner to where a woman stood over an open grill. She stared with longing and her mouth watered. She would give a week's worth of wages—if she actually got to keep any of her money—in exchange for one of those steaks seared over a fire.

"Come on, feet." She nodded with determination. One day. One day she would have the exact life she wanted. But for now, she had to hurry along if she didn't want to risk making yet another complete mess of things (like the lost necklace—which she deftly pushed out of her thoughts.)

She finally spotted the smithy and slowed. It was a plain building of wood slabs with two double doors—both closed. What had she expected, though? The man probably lived where he worked, and probably didn't wish the whole town to see him go about his morning routine. She rapped on one of the doors and took a step back to wait a good minute for the man to answer.

Nothing.

She knocked a second and third time, each knock growing progressively louder.

Still no answer.

What was taking so long? Had the man forgotten that she was to arrive today? Could he still be asleep? Really, though, could anyone actually slumber through such pounding?

A thought flashed through her mind and she gasped.

What if some ill will had befallen him? What if he was sick... or laying under some anvil, injured and unable to answer? She clutched her satchel.

What if he died? Worse yet... What if he died and she had done nothing to save him? Surely, she would be to blame. The town would think her some simpleton. Dona Ramirez would come up with some lousy excuse to not pay her—something about how simple-minded women didn't deserve to earn as much as others. She would end up working for the woman the rest of her life.

Never!

Mariposa wasn't about to wait around and risk the possibility of her life going from bad to worse. She pulled on the heavy door, the hinges loudly creaking and sunlight flooding the small workspace.

"Hello?" She asked and entered, surprised to find the place completely empty. Well, almost empty.

In front of her was the fire pit, now cold and waiting for the day's first use. She paid little mind to it and walked what did hold her attention—a row of swords all lined up along the back wall. She was astounded. Never had she seen so many in one place. Never had she seen such a variety, either. Some were straight as arrows; others curved like fish hooks that hadn't been bent completely into shape.

She walked over to a particular one that caught her eye and reached up to reverently touch it. Allowing the satchel to slip from her shoulder and fall to the ground beside her, she grasped the handle. Smooth, cool leather molded to her hand as if the sword had been made specifically for her. She lifted it, surprised at how it weighed more than she had expected as it dipped low, swinging towards the ground. She grabbed it with the other hand and lifted it back up.

"What are you doing?"

Mariposa swung around, the sword whipping through the air as she did.

Shin Bushido jumped back.

"Oh, sorry!" Mariposa cringed. Then she went through a string of emotions ranging from surprise to mesmerized. Jet black hair, dark brown eyes... The man who stood before her had been blessed with some of the most pleasant features she had ever seen.

Too bad his attitude wasn't as pleasing.

Shin rattled off a string of complaints similar to the ones she had heard her mother speak, but were still too foreign to completely decipher. The angry tone and hard look in his eyes were all she needed to know, though.

"I said I'm sorry—" Mariposa started to apologize once more, but then thought on it again. It wasn't her fault that the man had come up and surprised her! "Of course, that wouldn't have happened had you made your presence known like a normal person instead of sneaking around, trying to scare innocent women."

"Sneaking around? In my own smithy?" Shin choked. "Trying to scare—"

He tittered away in Japanese once more before pointing at her and falling quiet, his hands held up as if waiting for her to respond.

Mariposa shook her head. "You must be talking only to hear yourself speak, because I haven't understood a word you've said."

Shin's mouth dropped open.

"Yes, yes." Mariposa nodded. "I don't speak the language— a small fact Madame Fuku has obviously forgotten to share. Can we move on now? You look silly, standing there with your face like that."

Shin snapped his mouth shut and dropped his arms. His expression went from surprised to uncommonly solemn, and Mariposa suddenly remembered her assignment. She bit her lip, embarrassed. Once again, she had allowed her tongue to flap without thinking of the consequences for the words spoken. Women were to be submissive—especially a woman in her position. She forced a smile.

"My apologies... again." She looked down at the sword

that remained cradled in her hands and slowly lowered it. Remembering her mother's meek demeanor, she willed herself to abandon her natural tendency to charge ahead, and behave in a more agreeable manner. "Please, forgive me. I forgot my place."

She waited a long while, silently hopeful the man wouldn't demand his money back and then dismiss her. When several more seconds passed in silence, she finally glanced up. Head cocked to the side, he studied her intently.

"No," he finally spoke. "I don't believe you forgot your place at all."

It was Mariposa's turn to be surprised. "Are you calling me a liar? I am trying to be agreeable."

Shin smiled softly. "I'm not calling you anything. I'm simply saying that I don't believe the mild disposition you display now is the one you normally wear. Am I wrong?"

"You are wro—" Mariposa stopped before she could finish declaring that the man's assumptions were incorrect. However, that really would have made her a liar. She was many things—headstrong, stubborn, even boorish if given to the proper setting. A liar, though? She had far too little tack to successfully pull that one off. Besides, lies had a way of being dragged into the light—usually when most inconvenient. She sighed. "Oh, alright. I suppose you're right."

Shin's smile broadened. "I'll go out on a limb and say you probably aren't a wanted outlaw, either."

"An outlaw?" Mariposa asked, incredulous. "Why would you go and say a thing like that?"

Shin pointed at the sword she still wielded.

Mariposa smiled sheepishly. "Oh." She quickly lowered the sword. "I thought you were the outlaw—or someone else come to harm me."

"Do you have that happen often?"

"Have what happen?"

"Someone who tries to harm you."

She shrugged. "Not really, I suppose. A woman can never be too careful, though."

Shin nodded and reached out, taking the sword from her. She released it, clasping her hands together as she smiled wide.

"That's good," he said as he walked past her to place the sword back on the wall. "I'm glad to hear you're treated well at the okiya."

Mariposa gave him the look she hoped was the same as the one she received from her mother whenever she doubted something. It was a look that said, "I hear what you're saying. I just can't believe you're saying it." Could he really be so gullible? He certainly didn't look like the type who could have wool pulled over his eyes.

"I said no one was trying to harm me," she clarified. "That's very different from being treated well." Shin shifted with discomfort. Remembering Madame Fuku's words, Mariposa quickly moved on. "But that's nothing to worry about," her voice kicked up a notch, laced with false excitement. "I'll be free to do as I please once I earn enough to pay back the Madam. Speaking of which… I'm sure you didn't pay to hear me pass the time away. What chore would you have me do first?"

"Uh," he looked around as if confused. Had he not previously determined why he needed a servant before paying for one? He finally pointed down. "The floors. Yes, that's it. The floors could use a good cleaning."

Mariposa looked down to the dirt ground. The floors?

"So, you want me to sweep… the ground?"

"Yes… no." Shin shook his head. "I mean, I just want you to pick up any wayward pieces of metal customers might step on. Then you can clean the back room. That one actually does have floors—real ones. With wood."

41

He nodded resolutely, as if stating the obvious made his first suggestion to sweep the dirt ground completely reasonable. Who was she to argue, though? All that really mattered was that he paid for her services—which didn't seem to require much anyway. She shrugged. "Where will I find a brush and water?"

He pointed to a barrel of standing water in one corner of the room. A pile of supplies—a broom, rags, a brush, lye soap—had been placed beside it.

Hmmm. So, he had given some thought to the tasks he wanted her to complete. She picked up her satchel once more, walked over to the corner and proceeded to gather what she would need to do her work as he began his own. As she tidied up, he started the fire. The room quickly became warm—too warm—as she did her chores. Small beads of sweat dotted Mariposa's hairline. She mopped at her face, but continued to work the same as before, using the broom to swipe at cobwebs that had formed in various corners of the room. Meanwhile, Shin hammered away, occasionally dipping the metal piece into the fire, making it easier for him to mold it into the desired shape. Pleased with his work, he finished by dunking it in a large vat of water and set it aside to finish cooling. He fanned himself then and removed his shirt.

Mariposa stared for a moment, captivated first by the firm muscles that ran down his arms. Then the thick marks along his back caught her eye. She gasped.

Shin glanced her way, and she quickly averted her gaze.

"I probably should leave this on," he said as he forced one arm back into a sleeve.

"No, it doesn't bother me. Not that it would matter if it did. This is your place. I—I just wasn't prepared."

Shin smiled sadly. "Neither was I."

Mariposa debated whether or not to press forward.

Would he think she was being too nosey? Probably. It wasn't in her nature to avoid conflict, though. It would continue to bother her until she knew the answer. "May I ask what happened?"

Shin continued to put his shirt on, buttoning it as he walked over to where she stood near the water barrel. He dipped his hands into the water and splashed it on his face. "There isn't much to say. I failed my master. He reminded me to never do it again."

"Your master?"

Shin nodded. "Yes. The man who used to own this smithy. He brought me here—paid my passage from Japan."

Mariposa nodded. "I understand. A slave—like my mother."

Shin shook his head. "No. I wasn't a slave. Not really. I only had to work for him until I paid him back."

"But if a person can treat you any way they wish—even abuse you—and you can't leave... Well, isn't that the same thing?"

Shin thought about it for a moment. "Then I suppose we are the same, you and I."

Mariposa wanted to protest. She hadn't thought about it in terms of herself. She was born in Mexico, under the Plan of Iguala, which granted her the same permission as any other fellow citizen to enjoy equal political and social rights. However, she had been weaseled into a position of servitude. With the shoe on the other foot, she could see it now.

And she didn't like it.

"This conversation is too heavy for empty stomachs," Shin suddenly said. "And I'm hungry. How about we go into town? I smelled some delicious steaks on the ride in."

Mariposa hesitated. "Oh, um, okay."

"I know the food is probably much different than what we're used to eating. There is not so much fish around here."

Mariposa stood up a little straighter. "You seem to forget who I am and where I'm from. Beef is what we do in Mexico. Beef and chicken."

"Yes, you're right. I did forget," Shin replied as he started walking towards the door. Mariposa grabbed her satchel and followed him. "I suppose I'm having a little trouble reconciling the way you look with where you are from."

"Why?" She asked. "It shouldn't be so difficult. All you have to do is listen to the way I speak."

He smiled. "That is true. I suppose it is something of an enigma for me, though. I knew of fellow countrymen being sold to other people in places like Mexico. I just never personally knew someone who it had happened to."

"It didn't happen to me," Mariposa reminded him, her voice hard. "It happened to my mother."

"Yes, my apologies. That is what I meant. Sometimes I think one thing, but the words come out different."

"I understand," Mariposa replied as she followed him down the dusty street, and through the small town of Blessings. The smell of cooking food would have made it easy for her to figure out where to head if she wasn't already following his lead. "It was the same when I was younger. At first, my mother did try to teach me Japanese. She wanted me to have a connection to her home; to our ancestors. She tried teaching me English as well. Rather, the school that she worked hard to send me to taught me that. But then it became difficult in the community. People didn't understand my Spanish well. I would put together words from all three languages to try to communicate our needs. She decided then that it was too much—and that it didn't make sense for me to speak her language since we didn't live in Japan, and she had no intention of ever going back. She said my blood may have been like hers, but I was really a Mexican, and that a successful Mexican woman should be able to do trade with her own people and those who frequently passed through our city—the whites from up north. You see, slavery was abolished by the time I was born. So, there were less of our own people traveling to Acapulco.

"It must be a strange predicament you find yourself in," Shin noted as they arrived at the diner. "To be born free, but then to work for someone like Madame Fuku."

"Not for long," Mariposa said as Shin pulled out a seat for her. She sat and nodded her thanks as he took his own place across from her. "My plan is to work hard, work fast, and get out."

"Big plans back home?"

"Not particularly. I just don't like being under anyone's thumb."

"But isn't that what will happen anyway?"

"What do you mean?"

"You know... When you get married. You will undoubtedly follow your husband's lead."

Mariposa snorted. "And this is why I never plan on marrying. Too many men believe the same as you—that a woman was created to be some submissive creature, existing only to please man."

"That's not what I'm saying," Shin replied. Any attempt to further explain was cut off when the owner arrived at their table to take their order. Shin turned to his lunch guest. "What would you like to have?"

Mariposa looked around, uncertain. "Whatever you suggest, I suppose."

"Two steak specials," Shin requested. When they were alone to continue their conversation, he turned to her and smiled triumphantly. "You see? You did exactly what I predicted."

"What are you talking about?"

"I said you would follow a man's lead. You said you

wouldn't. But then you were asked to decide on something, and you gave me the choice to decide for both of us."

"That's not the same thing. I said I'd eat whatever you wanted only because I've never been here before. It was easier than questioning the poor woman to death, making her stand there and explain all her dishes to me when she has other customers to wait on. So, you see, I was doing her a favor." Mariposa clucked her tongue with irritation. "You know, you're quite infuriating."

"Ah, and now you know why I will never marry either. You have found but one of my many faults."

She rolled her eyes. "Enough silly banter about marriage. Obviously, we both agree it's a terrible idea. Tell me something else instead."

"Like what?"

"Oh, I don't know. Anything. I told you about my family."

"Only about your mother."

Mariposa crossed her arms. "Well, that's all you're going to get for now."

Shin chuckled. "You are stubborn. Probably the year of the Tiger—maybe the Dragon."

"The what?"

"You know. The sign you were born under."

"No, actually. I don't know," Mariposa admitted. "What exactly is that?"

"It's kind of like something that represents your personality. It's all based on the year you were born."

"Hmm. I'm not so sure I believe in all of that."

"No? I'll prove it. What year were you born?"

Mariposa frowned. "Are you sure it's not just a sly way of finding out a lady's age?"

Shin chuckled. "Come on. I will tell you mine."

"Alright then. When were you born?"

"1828," Shin readily admitted. "I'm a rat."

46

Mariposa cringed. "Yuck. That doesn't sound very appealing. Who wants to be a rat?"

"The rat is a very noble creature," Shin said with mock offense. "We are honest and ambitious and will work very hard for what we want. Oh, and we are also considered very charming."

Mariposa laughed. She quickly covered her mouth. "Yes, I can see that. It's ever-so-charming to brag about one's self."

Shin chuckled at her jest. "Alright. Your turn."

She sighed, but then smiled and shrugged. "1832."

"I knew it!" Shin hit the table, causing her to jump and nearby diners to look their way. He quickly lowered his voice. "I knew it. You are a dragon."

Mariposa gave him a smug grin. "That doesn't sound so bad. Not so bad at all." She held her head a bit higher. "We dragons must be strong sorts—able to take on anything."

Shin tilted his head side to side. "Eh... I wouldn't exactly say that."

"No?" Mariposa raised a challenging brow and her voice turned flat. "Then what are we?"

"Like I said—stubborn. Short-tempered, too."

"Ha! A real charmer indeed."

Shin chuckled. "Don't be upset. It's good that you're stubborn. True strength is like a sword—born of struggles forged in fire. It requires a bit of stubbornness. I believe that's the reason dragons inspire others."

Mariposa studied him. There was no pretense—only earnest intentions. It was, in fact, rather charming. She shrugged. "Perhaps there is some truth to what you said. If I'm honest—"

"And you are," he interrupted. "Dragons are always honest."

She smiled. "If I'm honest, then I like the idea of having

this sign you mentioned... even if I'm really a butterfly instead."

"A butterfly?"

"Yes. That's what my name translates into."

Shin thought about it for a moment. "I think they're the same thing."

"How so?"

"Butterflies fight hard to survive. As caterpillars, they must feed and then crawl out of the dirt to fight their way to the top of a tree or bush and build a cocoon. Then they have to do the hard thing of waiting for the right moment to break free from their prisons, claiming their rightful place in the world. I would think a fair bit of that requires determination." He smiled at her. "A bit of stubbornness."

The way he spoke filled her with a kind of emotion she hadn't known in a long time. It was like relief and inspiration and hope and desire... and so much more that she couldn't even explain. She wanted to tell him that—to thank him for giving her that little surge of energy that told her everything was going to be alright. She was going to be alright.

But their food arrived then, and in a rare moment, she did the least likely thing and fell silent. And so, they sat and enjoyed the moment of quiet company interrupted by nothing but the tantalizing smells of sizzling steaks and sweetened tea.

CHAPTER 4

"*I* like your collection."

Shin turned towards Mariposa, who pointed up at the wall of swords. He wondered how long it would take before she showed interest in them once more. All week she had been coming to clean the smithy, and he often caught her staring up at them, but she never said anything.

"Thank you," he said.

"Did you make them?" She asked.

"All but one," he admitted.

"Really? Which one?"

He walked over and pointed up to the same sword she had taken down the first day she arrived.

"Of course," she said, smiling. "It's very lovely. Who gave it to you?"

"The emperor."

"The... emperor?" Mariposa stared at him, her mouth open.

He thought to return her jest about how she looked silly standing there like that, but decided against it. They had gotten along well, and he did consider occasionally what it might be like to have her as an apprentice—should she be interested in the position. He most certainly could use the help. Orders for everything from shoes to bits, nails, hammers and more were piling up. Then there was the jewelry business he wished to start. It would be a viable business with all the gold and silver and precious gems miners were finding on a regular basis.

"You mentioned having a home the other day—a place away from here. Why would you not store such a beautiful gift there instead?"

"It is beautiful," he agreed. "But I don't wish for the constant reminder."

"You don't wish to remember how you were valued enough to receive a gift from an emperor? I once got a gift from my father—a man I didn't even know—and even though it reminded me of that fact, I would still wear it every day."

He looked at her hand, wrist and neck. "You said it was something you wore every day, yet I see no jewelry."

She glanced down, embarrassed. "I lost it."

"That's a shame," he said. "You didn't lose it here, did you? While you were working?"

"No, not here. Not even here." She gestured out the door, to the town of Blessings. "I lost it while I still lived in Mexico."

"And your search turned up nothing?"

"I don't mean I lost it like I dropped it or something." She sighed, a bit exasperated. Her voice dropped to a low mumble. "I lost it in a game of cards."

"What?" It was his turn to be surprised.

"I know. I know. It was stupid. It seemed like a good idea at the time, though."

"My mother had arranged a marriage for me. She said it would be good for me, because I would be well cared for.

The necklace was made of silver and gold, and it had a ruby too. It was worth a good deal and was to serve as my dowry." She closed her eyes and took in a slow breath before finishing. "I thought that if I won, then I would have enough money so to never need to marry anyone—especially someone I hardly knew."

"But you lost?"

She nodded, her face full of forlorn. "I should have known it was all rigged. No one ever beat the house before."

"I'm sorry you went through that."

"Yeah, well, I guess I got what I asked for."

"That's not true. You didn't ask to be taken advantage of—which is surely what happened if no one has ever won before."

"All the more reason I shouldn't have been so gullible. Someone like a rat wouldn't have done anything so risky, but worked hard to achieve his goals."

"I appreciate the compliment, but it's not true. A rat will work hard for their goal, but they are far from the clever monkey who makes wise deals. I, too, have made my share of mistakes." Shin took a moment to compose himself. "It's why I'm here in this country, and not my own."

"Did you lose your money or something?"

"I lost my post," Shin admitted.

"Your post?" Mariposa asked, intrigued. "What sort of work did you do?"

"I was a sensei—a teacher to the new students who would eventually become part of the palace guard. I was good at what I did, too. In fact, I was the youngest to ever earn such a position."

"What happened? Why did you stop doing something you obviously enjoyed so much?"

"Because I was relieved of my post. That's the nice way of saying it, I suppose."

"And the not nice way?"

"You saw the marks on my back?"

Mariposa nodded.

"I made the mistake of convincing the emperor's advisor that a foreign merchant who insisted on doing business in our country could be trusted. On my word, the advisor arranged a meeting for the man to meet the emperor." Shin sighed loudly and shook his head. "I should have been guarding the emperor, but I got distracted. The merchant tried to assassinate him."

"Oh, no. That's terrible! What happened to you? How did you become distracted?"

Shin fell silent. How could he say he had been turned by a pretty face? By his fiancé... who had turned out to be secretly working with the foreigner? It was too painful to even think about. He should have been more dutiful—more attentive to her needs. Then he wouldn't have failed both of them. He wouldn't have failed his emperor and his duty.

He deserved every ill will that had befallen his since.

"Another person," he finally said.

She eyed him suspiciously, and then shrugged. "Distraction is not my problem. It is my ability, or rather, lack thereof. I don't know how to fight."

"I know. I could see that by the way you held the sword."

"Hey!" She cried.

"What? Do you want me to lie to you? I'm not trying to be rude—only honest."

"Maybe you should try being helpful instead."

"I am," Shin replied. "I'm telling you that you need to practice."

"Practice what exactly? See, that's the thing. I don't even know where to begin." She gave him a challenging look. "Perhaps you should do more than offer your opinion, and try to teach me instead."

"Teach you? To do what?"

Mariposa threw her hands up. "To do what? What do you think? Cook chicken? Teach me how to properly carry a sword and how to swing it. Teach me how to fight."

Of all the confounded ideas! Shin shook his head vehemently. "Absolutely not."

"Why not?"

"For one, you'll hurt yourself."

"Not if you're teaching me!"

"For two, there's no time."

"What do you mean there's no time? I come here three days a week."

"Yes, to clean the shop."

Mariposa rolled her eyes. "Oh, please. Half the time I finish early, and the rest of the time is spent watching you work."

Shin suddenly saw an opening to his earlier dilemma. "I've been meaning to speak with you about that."

Mariposa blanched. Her eyes grew wide and fearful. "Do you feel you've overpaid for my services? Are you going to let me go?"

"No. Never. In fact, I've been quite impressed with your work. You do it well—and fast. You remember all the small details, too. It makes me wonder if you wouldn't be well suited for other lines of work."

"Other lines of work? Like what?"

"Like maybe trying your hand at metalwork."

"Metalwork?" Mariposa looked surprised. "I appreciate your confidence in me, but I don't see how I would ever be well suited for something like that. I could hardly lift that heavy hammer you swing even once, let alone repeatedly."

Shin chuckled. "No, I didn't mean that kind of metalwork. I'm talking about jewelry making."

"Jewelry making?" Mariposa smiled. "That does sound interesting. Would I be allowed to make whatever I want?"

"Kind of. You would get to design certain pieces to keep on hand—jewelry that served as examples of what we can do. However, you would have to make the jewelry customers paid for too. Some of them might have something specific in mind."

"Have you received those kinds of requests before?"

"Yes. In fact, I'm about to start working on one soon."

"What is it?"

"A ring for a friend's wife."

"Oh, that sounds nice. Will it be gold with little gems?"

"Most likely. It's meant to match another piece she already owns."

"Is it beautiful—the one she already has?"

"You know, I cannot say." Shin fell silent for a moment. Why hadn't Miguel brought him the necklace, or his wife while she wore it? Could he have been mistaken? Perhaps forcing a friendship where there actually was none? No, he didn't really think so. He was typically a better judge of character than that. Although, even he made mistakes sometimes.

His mind started wandering back to his homeland and how wrong he had been about certain associations then. Mariposa snapped her fingers and then waved a hand in front of his face. "Are you still here?" She joked.

Shin smiled tightly. "Her husband was to bring it by so I could get a look at it, and then design something to match. He hasn't been out yet."

"Maybe he changed his mind," Mariposa said.

"Maybe. He seemed interested when I suggested it, though."

"Then you should ask him."

Shin shook his head. "I don't want to come off as being too—what's the word—pushy."

"Why not? Everyone else is. That's how people get ahead in life."

"You don't really believe that. Do you?"

"Look at my situation. My mother was over me. Madame Fuku is over my mother... and now me—"

"Yes, the house mother seems a powerful woman."

"Not as powerful as Dona Ramirez, though."

"Who?"

"That's her associate—the woman who works with her, or works for her. I haven't quite figured out that situation yet."

"Huh. I don't know a Ramirez in town," Shin replied.

Mariposa shrugged. "I don't know her well either. I only know she was married to my father."

The admission hit Shin like a bucket of bricks. "Whaaat? What do you mean she was married to your father? I'm confused. What about your mother?"

He stood in shock as Mariposa swiftly churned out the story her mother had shared with her. Shin only shook his head. However, he couldn't shake a strange feeling that weaved its way through him. "How odd," he said. "Your father's wife is friends with the woman who knew your mother. What is the likelihood of that?"

"You're right. It is strange," Mariposa admitted. "I've been trying to figure all of it out for a while now—how it's possible that they know each other. Too, what it is that the house mother and Dona Ramirez are always whispering about."

"Whispering?" Warning bells set off, setting every nerve in Shin's body on edge. "Now that is suspicious."

"You see?" Mariposa grasped on to his arm. Her expression had taken on a look of real earnest. "These ladies probably have something crazy planned—maybe even something dangerous! That's why it's so important that I learn how to defend myself.

"Och!" A guttural sound churned from deep within Shin's throat. "You've tried to trick me."

Mariposa's features suddenly smoothed out into the picture of true innocence. "Trick you? I would never!" Using her index finger, she crossed an 'x' in front of her chest. "That's my solemn vow. Still, you should teach me how to properly defend myself."

"No."

"Oh, come on. You want me to learn how to work the metals, right? Well, I want to learn how to be a Kunoichi."

"Kunoichi?" Shin laughed far louder than he had intended. "Why, that's the silliest notion I've ever heard!"

"Why?" Mariposa defensively asked, her arms crossing in front of her. "I know they exist. My mother told me so."

"They do exist," Shin said. "However, not here—back in Japan. There's no real need for them. Besides, the Kunoichi wasn't all about fighting. I mean, don't get me wrong. They most certainly knew how to defend themselves. Physical fights weren't the first thing they turned to, though."

"Then how could they have been assassins."

Surprise hit Shin like a rug being pulled out from under him right before he landed on his back. Had he once again misjudged a woman? "You wish to be... an assassin?"

"What? No! I only want to know how to be that effective. That way no one would ever again take advantage of me. I would be like those warrior women.

Listening to her talk would surely have made any other man think she was insane, but there was something about it all that he found appealing. Was it the opportunity to teach again—to give him a small taste of the life he had lost? Or was it that stubborn dragon spirit he found endearing?

Endearing? Where had that thought come from? No, that was treacherous ground to walk on. He couldn't think that.

Although, she would never quit trying to convince him. Of that much he was sure.

Shin decided. "I will make a deal with you. If you promise to complete your chores and apply yourself to learning how to craft fine metals, then I will teach you the way of the warrior."

"The way of the warrior," Mariposa breathed. Her eyes glazed over with dreamy thoughts.

"Focus," Shin barked. She startled and he realized that his approach would have to be different from that of a palace, or even a temple. He softened his voice. "Focus. That is the key to success."

"I will," she said.

Shin made a fist with one hand, held it in the other and gently bowed forward. It didn't take long for her to copy him. He straightened back up and waited for her to do the same before continuing. "Normally, I would have you call me sensei. However, I think it would be too strange for us to begin now. Neither do I wish for you to continue to call me 'sir.' It will only be Shin from here on out."

"That sounds fair," she said. She flashed a smile. "So, when do we begin? Now?"

"Well, the smithy is tidied," Shin said looking around. "Although, I would hardly call this the sort of place one should train. There's not enough space. Still, the swords are here. I suppose I could do that much—show you how to properly hold one."

"Holding a sword isn't the problem," Mariposa countered. "It's the swinging that I don't know how to do."

Shin softly snorted. "Trust me. Holding the sword is the problem. When you know how to properly hold a sword, then it'll be easier to swing it."

He pulled the lightest sword off the wall and demonstrated by standing with his legs shoulder width apart.

"Alright. First, you want to find your balance—like this. Then you bring the sword up."

He stood beside her, slowly swinging the sword through the air. When he was finished, he stepped back and lowered the sword. "Now you try."

Mariposa stepped forward and grabbed the sword by the handle. "Oh, I like this one. The other is more powerful, but this is much lighter and easier to hold."

"Power is in the eye of the beholder."

She laughed. "I think you meant 'beauty.'"

"That, too." He smiled back at her, finding a sense of comfort in her enjoyment in something that he himself delighted in. Confidence reflected in her eyes, drawing him deeper into her gaze.

She abruptly turned, returning back to the practice at hand. "I can do this," she said and copied the same moves that he had shown her minutes earlier.

"Very good," Shin complemented her. "It'll be a little harder when facing an actual person, though. Not saying you ever will, but you should know that."

She shrugged. "I don't see how it will be that much different."

"It's the strike that will surprise you—the sudden thud as the sword meets a barrier and stops. It can be jarring, to say the least."

He looked around the room and pointed to one of the building's wooden support beams. "Come. Try it here."

"Here?" She asked. "You want me to hit the wood?"

"Yes."

She did as instructed, barely tapping the wood.

"With force," Shin demanded. "Fighting is for life. It is to save your life. When you practice, you are preparing. Prepare yourself to save yourself. You must remember that you have the power to 'wake from death and return to life.'"

Mariposa visibly swallowed. She had heard about the dead coming back to life, but that was only in the occasional church services she attended at her mother's insistence. Was Shin trying to say such a thing really existed—that he believed in it? "What does that mean exactly? A person can bring themselves back to life?"

He chuckled. "It means to take a bad situation and to make it a successful one. Now, do that for yourself and hit... your... mark."

She nodded and turned back to the beam and tried again... and again and again.

"Good," Shin said after half a dozen tries. "That last swing would have defeated your enemy."

"Ha!" Mariposa cried out triumphantly as she lowered the sword. "Now, no man will ever take advantage of me—not even a husband."

Shin guffawed. She was far from accomplished, but he wasn't about to tell her that. She had practiced hard, and he was well aware that students did better when praised then when needlessly pushed. So, he hung to her last words instead. "Ah ha! You do wish to marry," he joked.

"I didn't say that!" She screwed up her face with indignation, and then doubt. "Did I say that?"

"No," he eased her fears. And he couldn't help but wonder why he had said it to begin with. Really, he was allowing himself to feel too much emotion. It didn't matter how intriguing or beautiful—no, not that—intriguing or powerful he thought she was. He would have to practice more care, and refrain from getting swept up in her free-spirited ways.

She nodded resolutely before sticking a finger in his face. "Good. I don't need you going and getting any not-so-bright ideas." She wagged her finger back and forth. "There's absolutely no way I'll let anyone stick me in some cage like a canary—or worse—like those strange men who come to

Mexico, hoping to capture butterflies to pin in their collections."

Shin gasped with pretense. "I would never do anything like that."

"Ah ha!" She repeated him and stepped closer. "Then you admit it. You wish to marry me."

He straightened up. How in the world did she work that one out? More importantly, why didn't it bother him that she made such an accusation? If he was honest with himself, there was an attraction between them. However, it wasn't something that could be pursued. Even toying with the idea was irresponsible. He firmly shook his head. "Oh, this is silly. Perhaps we have been working too hard. Yes, that's it. I think we should take a break."

"A break? But why? I am not tired in the least." Mariposa deflated a bit. "If it's because of what I said, I apologize. I didn't mean any disrespect." Her eyes darted back and forth, as if trying to find a good explanation for the argument she had started. "I was only joking with you. I know you would never feel that way about me." She forced a laugh, and then lightly punched his arm.

He cleared his throat, unwilling to pursue the possibility of what her words suggested. "I know. It's just that it's the lunch hour. We should eat. Besides, it's like I said before. There's not much space here. Perhaps I can show you where I practice. It is much more suitable."

"Today?" She asked, hopeful.

It was his turn to wag a finger at her. "You are a sly one."

"I try."

He chuckled. "Well, you'll have to try harder next time. Don't think I've forgotten your other lesson."

"My other lesson?" She asked innocently.

He gave her his best I'm-not-fooled-in-the-least expression. "Yes, your other lesson. The one that requires bending metal instead of swinging it."

She gave him a sheepish grin. "It was worth a try. You're right, though. We had a deal and fair is fair. Show me how to bend metal."

"This way," he said and led her to her next lesson, hopeful she would enjoy it as much as he enjoyed teaching her new things.

CHAPTER 5

*M*ariposa stretched, imagining that the way she felt must have been much like the street cats she occasionally saw back home. They would lounge in sunny spots after a night of hunting (or whatever it was cats did at night), lazy and worthless. That's how she felt—but in a good way. The last time she returned to the smithy, Shin had decided that they had both worked hard enough around the shop and invited her back to his home. Well, not exactly. She didn't enter the main residence. Instead, she had been brought around to the small building off to the side of the main one. She wasn't sure what she was expecting, but it certainly wasn't "the place to find the way." That was how Shin had introduced it to her. It sounded very official and effective... or perhaps that was because of how he constructed the building.

A long, rectangular building made of wood with washi paper serving for the doors and windows, all of which could slide open. It afforded privacy while still keeping the room from retaining too much heat.

Mariposa smiled to herself. She had learned fairly quickly

how easily it was to become overheated while training. She thought she had experienced the worst of it within the smithy—which easily overheated because of the forge. However, the doors opened even wider in that building, and with the addition of water barrels, the place was even cooler. Too, Shin had not been training her nearly as hard as he could have while they were in the shop—not nearly as much as yesterday. She still ached from all the various ways she crouched and bent, and tried to support her weight with the strength of her arms—movements that were designed to help her muscles grow strong enough to easily swing a sword. She couldn't complain, though. Being a little sore was well worth all the training she was receiving—for both learning how to walk in the way of the warrior, and learning how to craft fine metal objects. Shin had yet to trust her with silver or gold, and she was still only on iron pieces. She would succeed at that as well, though. It all was a matter of time... and time was something she had plenty of in this place.

"Still in bed? Get up!" One of Mariposa's "sisters," Pearl, stormed into the room. She wasn't really a sister and Mariposa disliked the idea of them being associated as such, almost as much as she disliked the idea of having to call someone by a name that wasn't even theirs—especially when the individual didn't live up to it. But those were the rules of the okiya. The woman had been given an American name with the hope that customers would find her more attractive. Mariposa wasn't sure anything at all could make that woman attractive, though. Had they been sisters in real life, she really would've needed to know how to fight, because Pearl always acted like someone had spit in her tea.

"What do you want?" Mariposa grumbled.

"What do you think, you lazy thing? Your job is to help me ready for the day. There are customers waiting. You're keeping me from making good money!"

"Your sour disposition does that well enough for you," Mariposa shot back.

"Why, you little—"

The woman lunged at Mariposa, aiming to grab a handful of her hair. Mariposa easily slipped off the bed. In one smooth, continuous movement, she turned, crouched and stuck a leg out, effectively tripping Pearl.

The young woman toppled forward with a scream.

"What is going on in here?" A voice demanded, and Madame Fuku appeared a moment later.

"She tried to kill me," Pearl cried from her place on the floor.

"No, I didn't!" Mariposa argued. "She tried to attack me. All I did was defend myself."

Madame Fuku looked from one girl to the next, her dark eyes drilling into theirs. She finally settled on Pearl. "Is it true? Did you try to attack her?"

Pearl quickly went from sitting on the floor to kneeling. She bowed low until her forehead reached the ground. "Forgive me, oka-san. I forgot myself when she would not help me ready for Mr. Penderton. He has been waiting a long time. I was afraid you would become angry if I failed to fulfill my duties."

"Is this true?" Madame Fuku asked of Mariposa. "Did you refuse to help her?"

The two women stood in silence, staring at one another for what seemed like an eternity. "Stand," Madame Fuku finally said, addressing Pearl while keeping her eyes on Mariposa the whole time.

The woman did as instructed. Madame Fuku tied her sash around her waist, creating a large, yet delicate-looking bow. She gave Pearl a once over and then nodded her head towards the door. Pearl scurried away, but not before the Madame gave her one more order.

"Pearl, send for the boy."

The woman's eyes grew wide, but she still complied. "Yes, ma'am."

Mariposa crossed her arms. "You can't do that."

"Do you dare to tell me what I can and cannot do in my own house?" Madame Fuku asked, her voice dangerously low.

"It's not right."

"Perhaps you will think about that and consider the weight of your actions next time."

Mariposa was about to argue when a young, scrawny child of about eight years old appeared, accompanied by a young maiko who carried a slender piece of bamboo.

Madame Fuku took the bamboo from the girl and waved her off. "Turn around, boy."

She lifted the stick, ready to bring it down across the boy's back when Mariposa jumped forward. "No! I will take my own punishment."

"I can't hit you," Madame Fuku responded, as if the very suggestion was the most ridiculous thing she had ever heard. "Your buyer would not pay for broken merchandise."

"I won't tell," Mariposa insisted. "And I'll keep working the same as I have been. He'll never know the difference."

"Ah. So he is a man of some honor, and he has not yet touched you."

The very suggestion warmed Mariposa's cheeks. Her stomach fluttered with the thought of being intimate with any man at all—especially a man like Shin.

Madame Fuku nodded knowingly. "But it not because you haven't wanted him to."

Mariposa was left speechless. She shook her head.

"Do not deny it," the Madame said. "I can tell by the look in your eyes. You're in love with him."

"No," Mariposa insisted. "I'm not in love with him. I am in awe of him."

"In awe? Of a blacksmith?"

"He wasn't always such. He was once an important palace guard."

Madame Fuku cocked her head to one side. "Interesting. A palace guard? I wonder what happened to bring him to a place like this."

"I—I don't know," Mariposa lied. Her false words rang in her ears, and she thought quick to find any small truth to wash over the falsehood. "Sometimes I talk too much. I think it irritates him. He always turns quiet when I do that."

"Then perhaps it's time you learned to control your tongue, and allow the man to lead for once... or next time will turn out badly for the boy," she said and nodded at the child. He scurried away, apparent relief on his face. The Madame turned back to Mariposa once more. "You'll also do double your duties around the okiya today—and you will do them without fail. Am I understood?"

Mariposa gritted her teeth, but forced herself to comply all the same. She didn't wish to see any child hurt because of her rash decisions. "Yes, ma'am."

"Good. Now go."

Mariposa sped out of the room and down the stairs, almost bumping into Mr. Penderton being led back up the stairs by a less-than-enthusiastic Pearl. Mariposa felt somewhat bad for the young woman, and yet relieved at the same time that she had not been deemed worthy enough to be geisha. It was obvious only one thing would appease Pearl's customer at this point, making Pearl much less geisha... and much more like a woman from any number of cathouses that sprawled across the many surrounding towns.

She stepped aside and frowned, feeling a little guilty for the role she played in putting the young woman in the situation she was in. Maybe things wouldn't have turned out this way if she had just been agreeable and helped Pearl get ready. Then the gentleman wouldn't have waited so long, and maybe he wouldn't have needed to be appeased. At the same time, there was no guarantee of that. Sometimes the men who came in acted less gentlemanly than the rules of the okiya demanded—their act of gentlemanly conduct just that… an act.

Mariposa sighed as Pearl and the man disappeared into one of the rooms, the door shutting soundly behind them. Meanwhile, another door downstairs opened. Dona Ramirez stepped out and Mariposa pushed herself up against the wall opposite the staircase. If there was anyone she didn't wish to see, it was the woman who treated her more like property than even Madame Fuku. While the oka-san was demanding and could even be cruel at times, there was a sense of real violence that followed around Dona Ramirez.

She waited until the woman passed, too busy speaking to a man who accompanied her to pay any attention to Mariposa's little spot between the wall and staircase.

"You're a fool," Dona Ramirez growled. "I wouldn't be in this predicament if you had done your job to begin with."

"I did do my job," the man drawled. Mariposa squinted as she tried to get a better look at the man.

Turn around, she willed.

"If you did your job, then why don't I have the necklace? Why isn't it in my hand?"

Necklace?

"Hey, lady. I delivered as promised. You're the one who lost it after the fact."

"And then I paid you to fetch it once again," Dona Ramirez snapped. Her brows narrowed. "And you'll do well to remember exactly who you're speaking to. This 'lady' could easily have you dispatched… or have you forgotten?"

"How can I?" The man muttered. "You keep reminding me."

"Well, maybe you wouldn't need so many reminders if you would deliver as promised, Mr. Monroe."

Monroe!

Mariposa nearly gasped at hearing the man's name. She squeezed her lips tightly together. Could it be? Was it possible that the man she had lost the necklace to in the game of cards—the American who had played on behalf of the house—was here in the same town as she? But how could that be? And why? He obviously hadn't followed her. Otherwise, he would be in pursuit of her instead of talking to Dona Ramirez. That meant he was here due to some arrangement they had made together. But what for?

Could Dona Ramirez have had something to do with the loss of Mariposa's necklace?

One question after another plagued her thoughts—so much so that she was completely unaware that the pair had moved on while she stood there trying to figure out what was going on. She shook her head, trying to clear her mind.

She needed to talk to someone—someone who had dealt with questionable people in the past. Someone who might be able to help her discern exactly what was going on.

She needed to talk to Shin.

CHAPTER 6

*S*hin dropped the hammer and pulled his gloves off with a frustrated moan. His mind wasn't where it was supposed to be. It wasn't on his work. Instead, it was somewhere down the street, stuck someplace within the walls of the teahouse that he still questioned being much of one.

It was stuck on Mariposa.

He sighed. This was no good. How was he to run a business when he couldn't actually focus on his work? Strangely enough, the only time he could focus well was when Mariposa was present.

You would think it would be the opposite, he chastised himself.

She had such a tendency to ramble on while she went about her own set of tasks. Whether it was sweeping or dusting, or whatever other chore she took on, she chittered away in a manner that reminded him much like a butterfly. Yes, she was true to her name. Her conversations fluttered from one topic to another, in a manner that might seem unplanned or sloppy. Yet, she always brought the conversation back around full circle in the end—proving that there was a point to everything she said, and that it was all related.

He smiled. "An intelligent mind," he mumbled.

Perhaps that was the problem. The work he did was repetitive—even mundane. It wasn't bad work. But it could get tiresome... lonely. Having Mariposa around the smithy changed that. Maybe that was the real reason he had taken an interest in her to begin with. When he first saw her standing in the yard of the okiya, she had seemed as sad and lonely as he felt inside. Having her around filled a hole he hadn't realized was there.

And it only made it worse realizing it now.

"Hey, there, friend."

Shin jumped at the sudden greeting and spun around to find Miguel standing in the threshold, accompanied by a woman.

"Sorry about that," Miguel apologized. "Maybe we should have knocked first."

"No, no that's alright. I was only lost in my thoughts. I've had a lot of work of late."

"Oh," Miguel took off his hat and scratched the back of his head. "Well, then, maybe we should go. We don't want to bother you."

"It's no bother," Shin countered. "I asked you to stop by. Remember?"

"Yeah, that's why we're here."

"Then may I assume this is the Mrs. Santiago?"

"Aw, man. Where are my manners? Yes, this is my wife."

The woman stepped forward and held out a hand. "A pleasure to make your acquaintance, Mr. Bushido." She spoke with a voice coated in a soft Spanish accent. "I'm Araceli."

"Thank you for coming," he shook her hand. "And we are all friends here. Please, call me Shin."

"Thank you for inviting us, Mr. Shin. My husband has spoken highly of your work. He says your artistry with metals is equal to my own efforts with paints. I'm sure it is a misplaced compliment. Surely, it's much more difficult to mold metal than dabble in paints."

"I doubt that, but thank you." Shin stepped aside. "Please, do come in. I'm sorry I don't have tea or something to offer."

"Nonsense," Miguel said. The couple entered further into the smithy. "You're already offering us something incredibly valuable. Honestly, I'm still not sure if I should have accepted."

"Yes," Araceli agreed. "My husband told me about your offer to craft a ring for me. Honestly, I'm very flattered. However, I strongly believe artists should be paid for their work."

"Now, it is I who am flattered. I'm not so sure I should be considered an artist, though. My new apprentice seems to be exceeding even my high standards. Perhaps she will be the one to craft the ring for you instead."

"As you see fit," Miguel said. "Where is this apprentice anyway?"

"Yes," Araceli echoed her husband's curiosity. "I'd like to meet another artist."

"She only comes three days a week," Shin said, hesitant to add more. He wasn't sure how the Santiagos would feel to learn about who his apprentice was, and he didn't feel inclined to explain their unusual arrangement. There were already rumors going around town about the okiya. The good wives of Blessings had brought complaints against the "teahouse," demanding the "Today is actually one of her days—"

He hadn't even finished his sentence when Mariposa burst through the door. She doubled over, panting. "Shin."

"Mariposa." He wavered between her and the Santiagos,

trying to process both surprise and concern. "These guests are the Santiagos—Miguel and Araceli, respectively." He leaned towards her and lowered his voice. "What are you doing here? Is everything alright?"

Tears filled her eyes and dared to run over. She shook her head.

His stomach twisted at the dismayed look on her face. He motioned for her to walk past and onward towards the small room in the back of the smithy. "Excuse us for a moment," he said to the Santiagos while bowing slightly. Then he followed Mariposa, into the back room.

"What's wrong?" He asked as he entered, only partially closing the door to allow some privacy for their conversation, but leaving it open enough so that no one could accuse them of doing anything inappropriate.

"It's the man—the man who took my necklace. He's working for her!" Mariposa cried.

"Shhh," he tried to calm her. "It's going to be fine. Just calm down and explain it. I don't understand what you're talking about. What man?"

Mariposa took a slow, steady breath. "Remember how I told you that I lost my necklace in a card game?"

"Yes, 'to the house' is what you said."

"Right. To the man working for the house," Mariposa clarified. "Well, he's here… and it seems like the person who owns, or at least runs, the house is Dona Ramirez."

"Madame Fuku's associate?"

"Yes, that's the one."

"But how is that possible? She doesn't even live in Mexico. From my understanding, she doesn't even live here. Her home is in a neighboring town, Caldera. I can understand her doing business in Blessings, what with the mines and all, but what benefit would it be to go so far as to the far shores of Mexico?"

"I don't know. At first, I thought it was all revenge. I thought she wanted to get back at my mother for seducing my father—for taking him away and having me. But then I realized she sent that man, Mr. Monroe, to get the necklace and I couldn't help but think that's what it's been about all along."

"What could possibly be so important about that necklace, though? It must be worth a lot."

"Maybe. It's gold and silver—and it has a large ruby, too."

"Gold, silver... and ruby?"

"That's what I said. It's a gold and silver dragon claw clutching a rather large ruby. There's one other thing about the necklace, too. Actually, there are three things—three secrets."

"Wait." Shin rubbed his head. He slowly pushed the door open all the way and motioned for her to follow. "Mr. and Mrs. Santiago?"

"Back to a last name basis?" Miguel joked. He grew solemn then; ran a hand through his hair and cleared his throat. "We heard. We weren't trying to listen or anything, but we heard."

He held his hand out to his wife.

Araceli shook her head, one hand flying up to her chest. "How do we know she's telling the truth?"

"Come on, darling. What's the likelihood of there being two of those things in the world?"

"It's possible," Araceli argued. "What's the likelihood of both of them traveling so far from the same place?"

Her husband gave her a stoic look.

"My father gave me this necklace," Araceli continued. "It was a gift."

"Taken from someone who had first gifted it to his daughter?"

Araceli turned in defiance. "What are these secrets?" She demanded.

Mariposa, confused, looked to Shin for help.

"It might be possible that she has your father's necklace."

"But how?"

"What does it matter how if she can return it to you?" Shin asked. "Do you have a way that you can prove it's yours?"

Mariposa nodded. "The ruby turns."

"A lucky guess," Araceli said. "Anyone might assume that of an old jewel."

"Yes, but this one is different. If you spin it all the way to the right, a small pin pops out of the other end of the dragon's claw."

Araceli looked down. Her husband walked up to her and took her hand.

"Araceli?" He asked. "What is it?"

His wife reached around her neck. A moment later, she was tugging the dragon claw out from where it had hidden beneath her shirt. "She's right. The claw has a small pin."

"What?"

"I found out when we were nearly mugged on our way back from the art exhibition in San Diego. The man had grabbed at the necklace, but then pulled away like he had been hurt."

"I remember that," Miguel said. "I didn't know why, though."

"I figured it out once we arrived home. I went to take the necklace off and put it away. I accidentally pricked myself. My finger hurt for a solid week. I thought to mention it to you, but then there was the fever. Everyone was getting sick and the baby was coming soon and..."

Her voice broke.

"And then Jagara," her husband finished.

She nodded. "By the time everything was said and done, I hardly even remembered the necklace at all. That is, not until you asked me about making a ring to match it. I figured I'd tell the craftsman about it so he wouldn't injure himself. Otherwise, it simply didn't seem important."

Mariposa stepped forward. "Well, there is one thing that is important—and it's the fact that you weren't the first to be pricked."

"Why?" Shin asked. "What does it matter who was pricked by the ring first?"

"The letter my father sent with the ring explained about the hidden needle and for us to be very careful with it, because it had been dipped in poison."

"Poison?" The men chorused.

"Yes," she explained. "It was a precaution in case anyone ever tried to steal it. The man who tried to steal it... well, there's no telling what happened to him."

"You mean," Araceli raised a hand to one warmed cheek, "he's dead?"

"Probably," Mariposa confirmed matter-of-fact.

"But then why didn't I die?" Araceli asked.

"I don't know. Didn't you say you were sick, though?"

"Yes, but I assumed it was because one of the men who attacked us had a terrible cough."

"That's possible, but I believe the main reason you weren't adversely affected is because he took the majority of the poison first. There was very little—if any at all—left by the time you pricked yourself."

Araceli looked first from her husband and then to Mariposa. She slowly reached around her neck and unclasped the chain. "I guess this belongs to you."

Mariposa cupped her hand, smiling at the weight of the necklace once it was laid in her palm. "Thank you," she said. "It's the only thing I ever got from my father. A strange gift to give a daughter—a dragon claw—but I suppose it only made him more unique."

"I don't know," Araceli said. "There seems to be a lot of people interested in dragons of late."

Shin's interest peaked. "Really? How so?"

"Your father... you... the men who tried to rob us." Araceli thought for a moment. "There was a man at the art expo that showed some interest, too. The only thing is that he wasn't really interested in a necklace, though. He was searching for a dragon statue made out of gold."

"The golden dragon?" Shin asked.

Araceli nodded. "That's it."

Miguel snapped his fingers. "Hey, I remember hearing something about that. I think it was supposed to be part of some legend or something."

"That's right," Araceli agreed.

"I don't know about any legend," Mariposa responded.

"I do," Shin said. "It was a story I heard while I served as a palace guard. It was a story told to encourage loyalty and good faith. I could tell it to you if you wish."

"Please do," Mariposa said.

Shin smiled. His eyes took on a faraway look. "It's an old story during the days when there existed one hundred kingdoms. A wealthy merchant traveled them all in search of gold—it was his obsession. He would sell almost anything just to have even a speck of it. One day, he found himself in the seventh kingdom where he met another man. The man said he wasn't interested in purchasing anything. Instead, he wanted to become a merchant himself. The traveling merchant laughed and told him it was a tough business to always be on the road—that a man could not do it if he had a wife or children. The second man said that he had no wife for she had died many years earlier. However, he did have a daughter—the most beautiful daughter in all of the one hundred kingdoms. Of course, the merchant very much doubted this. He said, 'Sir, I have been to all of the one hundred kingdoms and have seen many beautiful women—from exotic dancers to royal princesses. You cannot say yours is worthier than all of them.' But the old man insisted that his daughter was the most incredible creature to have ever existed. So, the merchant said, 'Then show me this beautiful daughter, and if she is as magnificent as you say, then I will give you all my gold to marry her right now.'

So the man summons his daughter. She was brought before them and the man is astonished. The woman has eyes the color of peacock feathers—emeralds and sapphires—and hair like onyx. Best of all, though, is her golden skin. The merchant drops to his knees. 'Fair maiden,' he says, 'you are by far the most beautiful woman in all of the hundred kingdoms. Marry me and you will want for nothing.' The woman says, 'I will marry you, but on one condition. Every year, when the land receives its first rainfall, you must take me up the mountain that overlooks the valley of sun and shadow. There, I must bathe twice—once in the hot springs, followed by a dip in the cool river.'

The man thinks this a strange, but simple request. 'I agree,' he says and the marriage ceremony takes place at once. After they have eaten and drank until they can do neither anymore, he hands all his gold over to his new father-in-law and takes his bride home.

The first year, the merchant does as promised. He returns home from his travels only to take his wife on the journey for her bath. The second year, he returns and repeats it all again. He's a bit less enthusiastic about it, though. This arrangement has cut into his travels—and his earnings. He doesn't quite understand why she can't do like other wives, and simply heat water to take a bath at home... or splash cold water on herself from the privacy of their own spring. Still, he does it.

The third year, he is aggravated by the thought of continuing on his wife's silly tradition. He decides that he won't return. He'll continue selling his wares, and in so doing earns more than he ever has before. 'That will teach her good," he tells himself. 'She won't care where she bathes once she sees there is enough gold here to buy her own hot springs.' So, he heads back home to tell her as much. However, he can't find her anywhere once he gets there. He searches the entire house, the yards, and even travels to the neighbors. In fact, the only thing he does find is a statue of a golden dragon. He thinks it all very strange. So he gathers up the statue and goes to his father-in-law, who immediately cries out when he sees the statue.

'You did not take her to the springs,' the man said. 'Now I see where your loyalty and faith really lay. It was not to your wife, but to your money. That is why you did not take her to bathe.'

The merchant doesn't understand. What difference does it really matter where the wife bathes?

'Fool,' the old man says. 'How could you be so blinded by your greed that you could not see what your wife was made of? Her eyes were emeralds and sapphires; her hair like onyx and her skin like gold, for she was made of the most precious of these. The yearly baths were in magic waters that washed her clean of these things so that she could retain her human form. Now, you shall know her love no more, for a golden statue—no matter how finely crafted—cannot love you back.'"

Mariposa exhaled a shaky breath. "That's an incredible tale. You don't really believe it, though. Do you?"

"That there was an actual woman who turned into a golden dragon? No," Shin replied. "However, I very much believe the statue does exist. There was report of one sold without permission about fifteen years ago."

"Maybe that's it!" Mariposa exclaimed. "That was shortly before I received the necklace. Maybe my father had found the statue and sent the dragon claw as a clue."

"It's possible," Shin said. "Now if only we could figure out what that clue was."

"It's a shame there's not some wise old man to help us now," Mariposa continued. "Like the father-in-law from the story."

"Perhaps there is a way to find out," Shin said "If we could find someone to examine it, then they could tell us exactly how much it's worth."

Miguel's eyes lit up. "I know just the person. Old man Atherton. Owner of five mines, there's no one in these parts who know gold better than he does."

"He's right," Araceli agreed. "Mr. Atherton is an honorable man, too. He won't try to charge you for looking at it, or try to buy it off you either. If you'd like we could take y'all."

Shin turned to Mariposa. "What do you think? Are you interested in finding out more about this necklace?"

She stepped aside. "Lead the way."

CHAPTER 7

"*A*ny help is greatly appreciated," Miguel said after formally introducing Mariposa to the town mayor.

The man rocked back and forth in his chair on the front porch overlooking the far side of town. "Not a problem. Not a problem at all. Y'all get on with them chores you mentioned."

Miguel chuckled at the fact that the elderly man still addressed anyone younger as if children. Araceli smiled and took Mariposa in a surprising embrace. "I'm sorry we must leave. However, we do have the shopping to do, as well as other tasks before getting back to Raquel."

"She sounds like a lovely child," Mariposa responded. "I look forward to meeting her one day."

"So do I," Araceli said. Then she and Miguel took their leave, bidding the rest of their party goodbye.

The elderly town mayor stroked his long, gray beard. "Now, let's see what we can see about this necklace."

He held his hand out expectantly and Mariposa produced the jewel.

"So this is what's been causing so much fuss?" Atherton said as he carefully took it from her. He held it up and turned to the sunlight. "Mighty interesting," his words whistled through a lost front tooth. "Mighty interesting indeed."

"What is?" Mariposa asked, adrenaline rushing through her veins. She couldn't recall the last time she had been so excited. Add to the fact that she had been reunited with her father's gift, and she was on the verge of giddiness.

"Give me a minute, young' un."

The man pulled out a small magnifying class from his top shirt pocket and continued to study the ruby. A few minutes later, he finally spoke. "You said there was a secret about the ring, but did you know there are two? Something is stuck inside the ruby."

"I did notice some sort of shapes inside the ball, but I didn't know what they were."

"Look," Atherton said. He held the magnifying glass out to her and she took it. "Now lean closer to the light."

Holding the ruby between finger and thumb, she examined the glowing red ball closely. "There's something inside."

"That's right. In fact, there are three somethings inside."

"What are they?"

"On the right is a tiny crystal. On the left is an emerald. Between the two is what looks like a small mountain made of gold."

Mariposa stared in awe. "I can't even imagine someone being able to make something like this. How did they get it in there?"

"Very careful craftsmanship," Shin offered. "I've known of a few artisans who could create something that fine."

"Do you think my father commissioned one of them to make it?"

"The possibility did cross my mind."

"But why?"

Shin thought for a moment. "Didn't you say the necklace arrived with a riddle?"

Mariposa nodded. "It arrived in a sack of rice flour with a letter. The letter contained the riddle and some sort of document regarding warrior women."

"Do you have either of those?" Shin asked.

"No," Mariposa responded. "But I did memorize the riddle by heart. It goes, 'If you're brave, then hold up high the ruby red dragon's eye that worships light as its guide to mountain temples surrounded by Coyote man and eagle cries. There is where you will find two cold flowers that never die, but twist and turn and testify their secrets to desert butterflies.' I thought it very beautiful, though I never really did understand what it means."

"If you're brave then hold up high... If you're brave," Shin whispered the words to himself. "'Hold up high... light... guide... That's it! The ruby acts as a map—a sort of guide—to point you to where you have to go."

"For what?" Mariposa asked, bewildered. "What could my father have possibly hidden that he wanted me to find?" She turned to Shin. "You don't think he found the statue and hid it somewhere in the mountains. Do you?"

"I don't know," Shin replied. "Anything is possible."

Atherton cleared his throat. "Who did you say yer daddy was again?"

"Rigoberto Sanchez y Cruz. He was a Spaniard who once lived as an ejido in Mexico."

"A landowner, huh?"

"Yes. He sold off most of his lands to move back to Spain."

"If he moved back to Spain, then how did Dona Ramirez end up in these parts?"

Mariposa hesitated. "Honestly, I don't know."

Atherton continued to stroke his beard. "Didn't you say

yer mama knew that other lady, too? That Madame Fuku running the teahouse?"

Mariposa frowned. "If you'd like to call it that. I think it's more a house of ill repute, though."

Atherton's busy brows lifted high. "Oh, really? Well, that'll be another thing to add to my list of things to do. But fer now, let's focus on this one. You know what I think? I think yer daddy might've told yer mama that he was going back to Spain, but something made him change his mind and he came here instead."

"What do you think changed his mind?"

"I don't know. I think that's what the riddle's fer, as well as the map hidden within the ruby—which I think I understand."

"You do?" Shin and Mariposa asked together.

"Mm hmm." Atherton nodded. "To the east of Crystal Range and the west of Emerald Bay, there's a mountain we call Middle Mountain. We call it that because it's between two of the prettiest places in all of the El Dorado valley, but it's dry for as far as anyone knows. Betcha the last of my good teeth if you were to go to the assayer's office, you'll find out yer father staked a claim there."

"Then maybe we should go to the assayer's office," Shin suggested.

"I can't," Mariposa said. "I have to get back to the okiya. I've already been away far too long. Madame Fuku is sure to suspect something."

"Alright. I'll walk back with you as far as the garden. Then I'll head to the assayer's office to see what I can learn."

"Might want to catch up with the Santiagos again," Atherton suggested as he held out the dragon claw. "Araceli's father is the one who found the necklace to begin with. He didn't remember much at the time and handed it off to his daughter, but maybe telling him some of this will jog that foggy memory of his."

Shin nodded.

"What do you think?" He asked Mariposa as he helped her with the clasp. She marveled at how his nearness used to make her feel nervous. However, now she felt his quiet strength. It fortified her own resolve.

She turned and smiled up at him. "If you think it's a good idea, then we will do it."

They continued to gaze at one another, until finally Atherton cleared his throat.

"Well, what' cha young' uns waiting fer? Get one with them chores now."

CHAPTER 8

"*I* don't know. Maybe you shouldn't come any further." Mariposa slowed as she neared the backside of the okiya's property line. Thankfully, a grove of bushes separated them from the rest of the garden, making it difficult for anyone to see. "The garden might be empty, but it might not. I wouldn't want to take the risk that it's the latter, and put you in a bad situation."

Confound it! Shin sighed. How could one woman be so infuriating, and still endearing at the same time. Here she was getting ready to walk into the proverbial lion's den, and she was more concerned about harm coming to him.

"Mariposa, how can you worry about my situation? I'll admit that I used to think my lot in life was bad. I've met with hardships before. However, many of them were brought upon myself."

"As were mine," Mariposa said, her head hanging with apparent shame.

"Why? Because you tried to better your lot and made a poor bet?"

"A bet that took an unnecessary risk. You would have never done that."

"That's not true," he said and tilted her face upwards. He watched how her eyes danced across his face, almost as if searching for something. He smiled softly. "I've taken more unnecessary risks than I can count, and I've also shown cowardice by not taking the ones that mattered."

"Which ones?" She asked, her voice barely a whisper. Her eyes grew soft and Shin couldn't help but dip his head. Their lips briefly touched, but it was enough for him to know that he was making the right decision. He had known betrayal before. That didn't matter now, though. It was worth risking his heart for Mariposa.

He straightened back up. "We'll talk about it later. For now, only know that neither Madame Fuku nor her associate can harm me. You on the other hand…" He clasped his hands down on her shoulders and squeezed lightly. "Promise me you'll be careful."

She gave him a mischievous grin. "Only if you promise not to follow me any further."

Laughter tickled the back of his throat, but he contained it. The last thing they needed was for anyone to be alarmed because of a bellowing fool hiding behind a pair of bushes. "I promise," he said. "I promise, too, to do all the things we discussed. I'll stop by the doctor's clinic first, and explain how we may possibly need him as an alibi. Then I'll go to the assayer's office."

"And the Santiagos?"

"Yes, and I'll see them too. Although, I hear Araceli's father hasn't been doing well of late. Between the disappearance of his youngest, age and illness, it will be a miracle if he remembers anything at all about the day he came across your necklace—let alone the legendary golden dragon. I'll do what I can, though."

"That's all any of us can do," Mariposa said as she started to slip through a small break between a pair of bushes. "Take care," she said in a hushed whisper.

Shin disappeared from sight and Mariposa was left in the empty garden alone. She breathed in deep, the fragrance of cherry blossoms hanging above filling her lungs. Mariposa reached up to touch the lowest of the branches. Her hand swept over soft pink petals, catching a few as they fell off. She looked down and counted them—three for the three wishes she secretly harbored. One, to figure out the secret of the dragon claw necklace. Two, for Shin to remain safe as he went about his business. Three, to escape the okiya. However, the last was not going to happen anytime soon.

Rough hands grabbed her arms.

"What are you doing? Let me go," she demanded.

"If that's what you wish," Pearl responded before pushing her through the back door. She fell with a thud.

"What do you think you're doing?"

"What she was told."

Mariposa's head snapped up. "Madame Fuku, I'm sorry it took me longer than expected. The doctor said—"

"Save your lies, girl." Madame Fuku came to stand in front of Mariposa. She glared down, her lips turned in a snarl. "Now tell me the truth. Where is the golden dragon?"

"I don't know what you're talking about," Mariposa's voice quivered.

"She's a liar!" Pearl shouted. "She didn't go to the doctor. She was running off to be with her blacksmith. I saw them from my window. They were kissing!"

She glowered down at Mariposa, triumphant.

"I happened to run into him while I was out," Mariposa said.

Well, at least it wasn't a lie. She *had* run into him. She just left out the part about not seeing the doctor.

"Get up," Madame Fuku commanded. "Go to your room until I figure out what to do with you."

"What?" Pearl screeched. "I make one mistake and have to pay for it with every last inch of me—literally—but she sneaks around and gets no punishment at all? She didn't run into him. She ran to him. Can't you see? She's in love with him!"

"Quiet, girl. You forget your place," Madame Fuku barked. She turned to Mariposa. "Though I can't help but think she might be right. You're blushing."

Mariposa's hands flew to her cheeks. She couldn't hide her embarrassment, though. Nor could she shake the memory of the gentle kiss she shared with the man who had indeed claimed her heart over the last few weeks.

"Take her arms," Madame Fuku ordered. Pearl gladly stepped forward and jerked Mariposa's limbs back, linking her own arms around each elbow to lock them into place.

"What are you doing?" Mariposa cried.

"The same I do to any of my girls who have lain down without my permission."

"I haven't been with anyone!"

"We'll see if that's true soon enough," the Madame said and lifted Mariposa's skirts up. "Let's see if you're soiled."

Mariposa's blood surged through her veins. Instinct taking over, she kicked Madame Fuku, surprising both of them. The woman fell backwards with a cry, startling Pearl at the same time. With her hold loosened, Mariposa quickly got over her initial shock. She pulled one arm free. With it, she swung around and punched Pearl. The young woman gasped. Then she let out a terrific, ear-piercing scream.

With Pearl blocking the back door, a murderous look on her face, Mariposa turned towards the only exit left. She ran towards the sitting room where all the clients were normally welcomed... and right into Dona Ramirez with her henchmen.

"What have we here?" She asked, her voice laced with menace. "Get her."

Monroe lunged forward, missing his mark as Mariposa spun out of his reach. She stopped. Feet shoulder width apart; she bent low and raised her arms, ready to fight.

Dona Ramirez laughed. "My, my. It looks like someone's been learning how to do more than sweep floors."

"You never know when you'll have to dodge trouble."

"Oh, I'm sure you're faster than me. Then again, I'm not the sort to give chase," Dona Ramirez said. She reached into the large pocket of her skirt and pulled out a Derringer pistol. "That's why I always carry a bullet... and believe me when I say you won't dodge it."

Mariposa froze. Dona Ramirez waved the gun at her—a signal for Monroe, who moved forward and grabbed Mariposa by the arm. She slipped.

"What's this?" Monroe asked. He reached out and grabbed at the chain peeking out from beneath her collar. Yanking hard, he pulled the necklace off. "Why, hello. You look awfully familiar."

Dona Ramirez stepped forward. "Where did you get this?"

"I—I found it when I—"

"No lies!" Dona Ramirez spun on her and pointed the gun at her once more. "Where... did... you... get this?"

Mariposa sighed. What could it hurt if she knew? It's not like they had the necklace any longer. "The Santiagos— Miguel and Araceli Santiago."

"I knew it!" The woman crowed. "I knew when my men described who had stolen the necklace it was him."

"Stole the necklace?" Mariposa asked, wavering between dismay and anger.

"Yes. Apparently, there were some complications." She glared at Monroe.

"Aw, I told you that was a mistake. I can't help it if some of my men got a little rowdy. That's what happens when a man's on the drink."

"Which is why they shouldn't have been, but that's neither here nor there."

"Yeah, and what kind of man was he? He wasn't even willing to exchange the necklace for his own son's life."

Mariposa inhaled sharply. "Shin told me about that—about how a child went missing."

Dona Ramirez snorted. "Girl, lots of children go missing. Who do you think I have searching these mountains?"

"You use children?"

"Of course, I do. Some of these spots we've checked out are too small for grown men. Besides, men want money, whiskey and women. That can get expensive after a while. Well, not the last on the list, but certainly the rest. Children don't require hardly anything at all."

"But a baby? What good can a baby be?"

The woman shrugged. "The baby was meant to serve as a trade. In fact, I sent a letter stating as much." She shrugged. "He failed to respond."

Mariposa shook her head. From what she remembered, it was Miguel who received the letter. And he only knew how to speak Spanish—not read it. "I don't think he ever got it," Mariposa said. "I think it was sent to his son-in-law instead."

Dona Ramirez cast a side glance at Monroe and he shrugged. "What does it matter who got the letter? You got a new son."

She stared at him a moment longer, as if deciding if the rewards outweighed the risks. "You're right. It no longer matters. He's mine now."

"But you already have a son," Mariposa argued. "My mother told me so."

"Had," Dona Ramirez corrected. Her face twisted with anguish. "Why do you think I've searched so long and hard for this stupid statue? After your fa—my husband passed away, our son went searching for the statue. Maybe he found it and ran off with his gold, but no. I doubt it. Not my Antonio. He wouldn't do that to his mama. Something surely happened to him, chasing after something so foolish. I told him just that, too, that I thought it a fool's quest, but Madame Fuku was willing to pay him well. He was like his father in that way. He liked money."

"Madame Fuku?" Mariposa spun around.

The other woman stared at her triumphantly. "Yes, girl. I'm the one in search of the golden dragon."

"But I thought Dona Ramirez—"

"Was married to the man who was my partner—who helped me steal the dragon."

She may not have known her father well, but she did remember the good that her mother spoke of him. Any man who would try to provide for a daughter society said shouldn't even exist, could not have been all that bad. Mariposa seethed. "My father would never do such a thing. He was honorable."

The Madame laughed. Her face distorted with sadistic humor. "Honorable? A married man taking on a lover— leaving her with child? Why do you think I allowed your mother out of debt? Passage to Mexico was not cheap. She would have worked for me the rest of her life—the same that will happen to you. Unless, of course, you help me find where he hid the statue."

Mariposa clenched her fists. She didn't care what either of these insane women said. She would find a way to escape.

She looked the woman square in the eyes and growled. "I would rather die."

"And so you will," Madame Fuku said. "The same as anyone else who gets in my way—including that precious blacksmith of yours."

Mariposa froze. She didn't mind giving her life for a righteous cause. However, the suggestion of Shin dying forced her to reconsider the Madame's demands. She was a snake—a serpent that quietly waited until the perfect moment to strike. That's how she had managed to appear less threatening between the two matrons, both of whom stared at her now with expressions of triumph and expectancy.

There was no choice. Mariposa didn't even want to entertain the idea of the people she loved hurt. She would sacrifice the dragon if she had to.

She would sacrifice her very soul.

CHAPTER 9

"You were right, Sheriff. There's no one at that teahouse. Well, not the people we're searching for anyway," the deputy reported. "There were a couple of ladies watching over the place. They didn't mind sharing what they knew for a few bills. Seems like that Ramirez woman and the Madame took Mariposa up to Middle Mountain—looking for gold is what the girls said."

"Hmmm. Makes me thankful we thought to gather a posse. Those mountains aren't exactly the greatest place to be right now. Lots of wildlife waking up, enjoying the warm weather."

Shin fought to remain composed, but his insides were filled with turmoil. He was worn through with worry, and overwhelmed by the number of people who felt the same. After visiting Doctor Jonathan Edwards and explaining his situation, the man insisted that they notify the law… and a whole lot of others. Shin scanned the group of people who had assembled to help, his throat tightening with emotion to see so many. He knew he had a friend or two in town. Never would he have guessed how many people actually cared, though. The sheriff and his men wore concerned looks. Doc Edwards and his wife, Kela, stood with a small band of Miwok warriors—warriors who looked ready to take on the armies of every nation. Even Miguel was itching for battle in his own way—hat low, loaded guns swinging on his hips, ready to set fire to anything that got in his way.

Shin wished he felt as confident as they looked, but a small seed of doubt sprouted in his mind. It was a terribly powerful thing. Doubt had cost him the life he knew—the one he had trained for as a sensei. Doubt had taken root in his mind—caused him to second guess himself and trust liars. If he was honest with himself, it was the real reason he lived such a quiet life now—the reason he believed there were so few who would stand with him. But this posse proved otherwise.

No, he couldn't go down the path of doubt again. He could trust these people.

"Do you really think they'll go up the mountain, and that we'll find them if that's where they are?" He asked.

"No one knows these mountains better than the Miwok." Doc Edwards said, draping an arm around his Kela's shoulders. "And I have every confidence that my wife's people will find them."

"That's right," Sheriff Pete concurred. "You couldn't be in better hands." He turned to the Santiagos. "And neither could you."

"I should be going too," Don Arroyo groused.

"No, father. It's too dangerous," Araceli said. "Besides, if what the sheriff suspects is true, then you have to go with them."

Don Arroyo sighed with resignation. "Do you really think you've found him?"

Pete nodded. "We've been searching into your son's

disappearance for some time now. More recently, we've started looking into Dona Ramirez too."

"Why?" Don Arroyo asked. "What made you think her a possible suspect?"

"Too many coincidences. Her own son passed away only a couple of weeks before Jagara's disappearance. She lives in Caldera, but helps operate businesses in all the neighboring towns—towns in which children have started to disappear, and the only connection is her."

"You think she might be taking them."

"If not taking them herself, having someone else take them. If what I'm hearing about this statue is true, it's probably worth a lot of money. The children that have gone missing aren't like Jagara. They aren't babies. It's more likely that situation was something personal. The other children all range from six to ten. If she's searching mines for that statue, then it would make sense to use a child. They're cheap labor that are, sad to say, easy to dispose of."

"And this Madame Fuku is no better," Shin added. "I know her teahouse isn't a true okiya. She is not trying to bring our culture to the people, but exploit those women. She might be involved in other crimes, too."

The sheriff's eyes narrowed. "How so?"

"You spoke of coincidence regarding the Ramirez woman. I can't help but wonder the same about Madame Fuku. What is the likelihood that she would open a teahouse with a woman who seeks the statue? Who is more likely to even know about it, let alone want it? From what Mariposa told me, Madame Fuku used to be in the business of transporting slaves—that's how her mother ended up in Mexico to begin with. I'm sure people weren't her only cargo."

"You thinking she stole the statue from your country?"

"If you look at it like a puzzle, then it makes sense. She is the only one connecting all the pieces together."

"Then she's more dangerous than I gave her credit for, and we shouldn't waste any more time talking."

The group agreed and the sheriff gave his orders. "Miguel and Mr. Bushido will follow the Miwok up to Middle Mountain while my men and I ride out to Caldera and see what we can find out. Don Arroyo, you and your daughter will stay here as eyes and ears. Make sure no other children go missing."

"As God is my witness, they won't," Don Arroyo swore.

"We'll stay with them," Doc Edwards offered. "And get the clinic prepared for whatever you may find."

Kela nodded her agreement. "If what you say about the disappearances are right, then we will need to make medicine."

"Emily will help us," the Doc said, referring to his former housekeeper who was now busy keeping house for her own family. "I'm sure she and Ukchuu will want to know."

"They know," Kela said. She gave her husband a wily smile. "I am a medicine woman with a trained owl. Did you forget?"

Her husband smiled back. "How could I forget?"

The couple shared a brief moment, and though it was hardly noticeable, it was there for any watchful eyes to witness. With every sense heightened, Shin couldn't help but catch the exchange. It filled him with hope and desire—hope that he would know such satisfaction one day, and the desire to find Mariposa and make it so. It also reminded him that the days he spent training her meant nothing if he was not going to take his own advice.

It was time to "wake from death and return to life."

CHAPTER 10

The sound of eagle cries overhead caught Mariposa's attention. Shielding her eyes, she scanned the horizon. The birds majestically circled overhead. How could such a small creature exert so much energy and yet continue to soar? They had been walking for hours and she was exhausted to the point of passing out.

"Maybe we'll never find it," she mumbled.

"If you don't have anything good to say, then don't speak at all." Dona Ramirez snapped as they neared yet another cave. It was the third one they had come to. She suddenly stopped. "Look!"

Mariposa and the men Dona Ramirez had hired to go with them all stood back and watched as the Dona pointed out an interesting carving made on the outside of the cave entrance. It appeared to be two flowers, their vines twisting around one another.

"Remember the riddle?" Dona Ramirez asked.

How could she forget? Dona Ramirez had made her recite it more times than could be counted on the ride over. It was enough to make her wish she had never heard of the golden dragon, or even receive the necklace to begin with.

"Alright," the woman said as one of the men lit a torch. She took it and then held it out to Mariposa. "You go first."

"Me?"

"That's right. Think of it as atonement for your father's sins. You would have never been placed in this kind of situation had he not had an affair to begin with."

And I would have never been born, Mariposa thought to object. However, she knew that mattered little to anyone there. They wouldn't care if she died on this mountain in search of this foolish pursuit. How she wished she could give them a piece of her mind... and a small taste of steel, too! She wasn't delusional, though. She knew she couldn't take on three men and la Dona all at the same time. Shin had taught her how to throw a punch, and even block them, but she wasn't some supernatural force to be reckoned with. With Monroe's gun jammed into her back, she had no choice but to obey. Mariposa yanked the torch away from Dona Ramirez, the fire no match for the anger within, and marched forward.

THREE HOURS OF CLIMBING reminded Shin how heavy a sword could weigh on one's back—a greater feat when walking uphill when compared to riding a horse. It hardly fazed him, though. If he had to, he would climb all the way to the heavens. Whatever it took to find Mariposa... which he hoped would be soon.

"Here!" Tuweeyu, one of the Miwok warriors, pointed to where twigs had been bent. Then he pointed to a cave entrance a little further up. "The ground is disturbed here. I am certain that's where they went."

Two other Miwok braves went to investigate. They returned a few minutes later and concurred that they were in the right place.

Miguel drew one of his pistols. "Then let's go."

"No," Tuweeyu said. "This is a dangerous place. It is Coyote-man's land."

"Coyote man?" Shin asked, confused.

Tuweeyu nodded. "Yes. O-let'-te is a god of many things —creator, ancestor, and sometimes trickster."

"I understand," Shin said. "I respect your beliefs and understand if you cannot go. However, I must ask you to respect mine. I believe in the *kami*. They are the spirit of every aspect in life—even the wind and the sun, and even this mountain. They are *my* ancestors, and I have to believe they know I am here only to do good. They will help me."

The Miwok braves exchanged glances. Tuweeyu nodded his approval. "Then we will wait here—call to O-let'-te to help you and your friend."

"Thank you," Shin said and started for the cave.

Miguel followed, stopping briefly to turn around and address the Miwok. "I'd wish you men good luck, but something tells me you won't need it."

They smiled at one another and Miguel disappeared into the cave with Shin.

"THERE!" One of the men pointed to a large crevice in the far side of the cavern wall. "There are those flowers we saw carved out front."

Mariposa stood in awe with the rest of the group at what appeared to be a dead end. However, light shone from above and revealed a small opening where water trickled down the rock wall. On either side of it were vines decorated with flowers. They were much like the desperado said, looking like the ones that led them here to begin with.

"You're right," Dona Ramirez agreed and she walked towards it. "It must be inside that small crevice. It'll be a tight squeeze, but I'm sure we can—"

"Watch it!" Monroe yelled and lunged at her, pulling her back as she started to slip. He raised his own torch and held it forward to reveal a pit. "I don't think you'd want to fall down that."

"And I won't," the Dona said. "Because I'm not going to be the one to cross over. She is."

Mariposa inhaled sharply.

Monroe nodded. "She would have a bit of a climb, but she looks sturdy enough to do it. We'll tie her to the end of a rope, let her down a bit and swing her to the other side. She climbs up, enters and retrieves our statue—I mean Madame Fuku's statue."

"*My* statue," Dona Ramirez corrected him. "Do you really think I'll give that woman anything after all the trouble she's caused? My family would have never been in this mess if it hadn't been for her and her stupid slave trade." She dug into a satchel that one of the men carried and turned to Mariposa. "Get on with it, girl. Tie this to your waist."

"No," Mariposa said.

"Now!" Dona Ramirez yelled.

"Or what? You'll kill me? Then you'll be no better off than before."

Dona Ramirez smiled. "True. I wouldn't be any better off —for a while. Then I would go and find one of those children I told you about. They're even smaller and easier to swing. Yes, perhaps we'll do that and just toss you in the pit now."

Mariposa swallowed. "No, I'll do it."

The woman smiled. "I knew you'd see things my way. Now, tie it on."

Mariposa took the rope from the woman and made a knot of it around her waist. Monroe grabbed the other end.

"Hold on to this," he instructed his men. He turned to Mariposa. "Go on. Climb down. We've got this side."

Mariposa knelt down on the ground. She exhaled pent up breath she hadn't realized she held until she was ready to swing over to climb down into the pit.

"A little more rope," Monroe called out. The men slid her down a little farther. "Stop!" Monroe yelled. "That should be enough. Now, push off the side of the wall and swing over to the other side."

Grimacing, Mariposa braced her feet against the wall and pushed. She swung out from the wall, bottling a small shrill in the back of her throat that threatened to escape. She made it halfway and then swung back.

"Again!" Dona Ramirez demanded. She held the torch over the pit and stared down at Mariposa. "You were almost there. Push harder next time."

Mariposa braced herself once more. Clenching the rope, she grunted as she pushed off the second time. She swung close to the opposite wall and reached out. Her fingers scraped the rockface before she swung away once more.

"Again!" Dona Ramirez screamed.

"I can't," Mariposa panted. "I've tried. It's too far. I can't reach it."

"Try again!" Dona Ramirez barked. She turned to Monroe. "Swing her harder this time."

"Or don't swing her at all!" A voice shouted from behind them.

Dona Ramirez spun around to find Miguel with pistol in hand. Shin withdrew his sword from its shield.

"Let... her... go."

Dona Ramirez clucked her tongue at them. "Boys, come

now. You're not really going to shoot at us. If you do, then she'll fall. Is that what you want?"

The two men glanced each other.

"Do it, Shin!" Mariposa shrilled. "Let me fall!"

"She's insane!" Dona Ramirez exclaimed. "She'll die if we let her go."

Shin turned to Miguel. "She's not insane. I trust her."

"That's all the 'go ahead' I need," he said and shot at the ground between the men and Dona Ramirez, who screamed as she dove behind a large rock, still clutching the torch.

Monroe and the other men jumped to the other side, the rope slipping from their hands. Still, they held on tight... until growls entered their space.

"What the—"

Shin and Miguel pushed their bodies up against the wall, trying hard to avoid the three coyotes that had just arrived. The beasts snarled at them, but continued walking towards the desperados instead. They bared sharp teeth and the men let go of the rope.

"No!" Dona Ramirez screamed. She lunged at the rope, grasping at the tail end with one hand. She rolled forward, towards the pit, the torch flailing and falling before the earth swallowed them both.

"Dona!" Monroe yelled and peered over the edge. The coyotes snapped at him and he jumped, pinning his backside against the wall. He slowly edged his way around them. Then he and the other men with him took off running, the coyotes giving chase as they ran back out of the cave.

"Mariposa!" Shin called and ran to the edge of the pit. He peered down. She had untied the rope from her waist and clutched the rocks several feet down. He looked back to Miguel. "Hold my legs!"

Miguel shoved his pistol back in the holster and ran over.

Both men lay on their stomachs, Shin hanging halfway over the ledge.

"Grab my hands," he told Mariposa.

Grunting, she slowly pulled herself up a few inches. She seized one hand and then the other.

"Pull!" Shin yelled back to Miguel as he did the same. Mariposa slowly slid upward, back towards safety until they pulled her over the edge. She landed on her stomach with a thud.

Shin stood and reached down to help her up.

"Thank you," she said. Then she stood and peered down into the pit. "Look."

The men approached. There, below where the torch dimly lit the bottom, laid two bodies.

Mariposa stepped back. "Something tells me mother and son have been reunited."

Miguel shook his head. "What a waste. All for some legend that's probably not even true."

"There's only one way to find out," Shin said. He glanced down at Mariposa and wrapped his arms around her. "If you want to."

Mariposa stared back up at him.

"Uh, I think I'll just find my way back out," Miguel said, shifting as he looked away from the couple. "Holla if y'all need anything."

Shin smiled and turned his attention back to Mariposa. "So, what do you say? We could always try going out, climbing up the mountain, and then back down onto the other side. That's probably how your father got there to begin with. That is, if it's really hidden there. It's a risk, but it's one that comes with great wealth."

Mariposa stared at the crack in the wall for a long minute. A slow smile spread across her face as she turned back to him. "Butterflies are not born for the love of gold.

They prefer protective shelters, because they understand that only a life of struggle will help them transform into something beautiful."

Shin brushed a stray bit of hair from her face. "You are that something beautiful, Mariposa. You always were." He lifted her face towards his and placed a gentle kiss on her lips. "Come. Let's go home."

EPILOGUE

*I*t wasn't exactly the kind of wedding one would have expected—not traditional by any means. There was a small shrine to represent the ancestors, but there was no Shinto priest. Far too many people were in attendance for what would have normally been a small, private affair. There were the nuptial cups, but no sake to share, the cups instead filled with spring water. The only thing that would have been considered in keeping with tradition was the bride herself.

Dressed in a white kimono, Mariposa met her husband as a single woman for the last time. Together, they exchanged smiles and secret glances, promises, and the sweet knowing that their lives together would be peaceful—that the *kami* or God or whatever it was wherever faith dwelled, had seen to it that those who wished them harm had been removed from their paths.

Madame Fuku had been found guilty for many crimes, and had been returned to her country to answer for the first of them (and probably for the rest as well).

The sheriff and his deputies did indeed discover a smuggling ring in the town of Caldera. They returned many children to their rightful homes, including Araceli's brother, Jagara.

As the only living Santiago, Mariposa inherited all that once belonged to her father. Having no desire to live in a sordid town like Caldera, she sold off everything. Everything except the dragon claw necklace, of course.

As her mother prepared her for the reception, helping her slip out of the kimono and into the more colorful *uchikake* silk robes, she undid the clasp of the necklace.

"Mother, I believe this is for you."

"No, child. That was a gift to help bring you great wealth."

Mariposa held her mother's hand. "I was always wealthy. I had you as a mother. I'm sorry I didn't tell you that sooner."

Her mother's eyes filled with tears as Mariposa reached around and put the dragon claw necklace on her. Then, in a rare moment of affection, she embraced her mother.

"Go on now," the woman said, her voice wavering. "Save that for your husband."

Mariposa smiled broadly, but nodded her consent. She turned back to find Shin waiting for her.

"Things seem to be working out well with your mother," he said.

"Yes. Although, I think I may have overwhelmed her. The necklace may have been a bit much."

"To be honest, I'm surprised you gave it away. After all you went through to find it."

Mariposa shrugged. "What use is a dragon's necklace when you are the dragon?"

"Wait a minute. I thought you said you were a butterfly."

Mariposa looked at him slyly. "And what do butterflies do?"

Shin squinted, studying her for a moment. "Transform?"

"Exactly," she said. "If I believe it, then I can achieve it. I can be anything I want, if I put my mind to it."

"And what is it you want to be right now?" Shin asked.

Mariposa gave her husband a mischievous grin. "Your wife."

Shin took her in his arms. "Sounds good to me."

Then they shared a kiss with just enough fire to promise a life full of passion.

A LETTER TO READERS

Writing this book left me feeling elated… and a little sad, too. It always feels good to finish a book—like I'm challenging myself to do something daunting and (amazingly) succeed at it. I can't help but think about my characters in the same light. When I write the heroine's story, I see her trying to accomplish a task that seems impossible or maybe even futile. Still, she does it in the end. She overcomes her demons and wins the day.

I like to think we can all do that. We can all "win the day." Sometimes those wins will be small—we got to work on time or didn't burn the food. Other times, we win big. This book —this entire series—was a big win for me. It was the first time that I really pushed myself to get out of my comfort zone. I had to do a good deal of research and find out about the cultures of others—friends and family who wanted to see themselves as their ancestors were back in the Old West.

I hope these books did justice.

Best,

Mimi Milan

P.S. Reviews are a great way of letting authors know that you would like them to keep creating. If you enjoyed reading *Birth of the Butterfly* (or any of my books), then please visit my page here and leave a review for me. Then sign up for my newsletter on my website at www.mimimilan.com to find out about new releases, freebies and so much more!

Stories like...

www.ingramcontent.com/pod-product-compliance
Lightning Source LLC
Chambersburg PA
CBHW020414130626
46549CB00006B/2551